# A Promise to Keep

# A Promise to Keep

## Mario Bencastro

### Translated into English by
### Susan Giersbach-Rascón

PIÑATA BOOKS
ARTE PÚBLICO PRESS
HOUSTON, TEXAS

This volume is funded in part by grants from the City of Houston through the Cultural Arts Council of Houston/Harris County and by an award from the National Endowment for the Arts, which believes that a great nation deserves great art.

*Piñata books are full of surprises!*

Piñata Books
Arte Público Press
University of Houston
452 Cullen Performance Hall
Houston, Texas 77204-2004

Cover design by Eclipse Design Group
Cover art by David Rosales

Bencastro, Mario.
   [Viaje a la tierra del abuelo. English]
   A Promise to Keep / by Mario Bencastro ; translated by
Susan Giersbach Rascón.
   p.   cm.
   Summary: Sixteen-year-old Sergio, struggling to honor his grandfather's wish to be buried in El Salvador, undertakes a journey filled with unexpected disasters, triumphs, and the memory of his beloved Abuelo.
   ISBN-10: 1-55885-457-6 (alk. paper)
   ISBN-13: 978-1-55885-457-4
   1. Hispanic Americans—Juvenile Fiction. [1. Hispanic Americans—Fiction. 2. Family life—California—Los Angeles—Fiction. 3. Self-perception—Fiction. 4. Grandfathers—Fiction. 5. Voyages and travels—Fiction. 6. Los Angeles (Calif.)—Fiction. 7. El Salvador—Fiction.]   I. Rascón, Susan Giersbach.   II. Title.
PZ7.B4307Via   2005
[Fic]—dc22                                             2005046494
                                                              CIP

♾ The paper used in this publication meets the requirements of the American National Standard for Information Sciences—Permanence of Paper for Printed Library Materials, ANSI Z39.48-1984.

5 6 7 8 9 0 1 2 3 4          10 9 8 7 6 5 4 3 2 1

*To Sergio Raúl Magaña,
in memoriam.
To Sergio Benjamín Castro,
survivor of two worlds.*

# Acknowledgments

My most sincere thanks to everyone who, with their ideas and enthusiasm, contributed to the preparation of this work, especially the select group of students and alumni of Belmont High School in Los Angeles and the students of OnRamp Arts, who participated actively in order that their voices would be part of this novel.

# 1

We buried Grandfather one week ago. The old man had just turned eighty. We were told he died of a heart attack, but no one in our family was sure of the true cause. What happened is that one morning he didn't come to breakfast, and my mother went to his room and found him sleeping. She shook him hard, and when she couldn't awaken him she began to scream desperately. We called the ambulance. The vehicle came to our house, the sound of its siren filling the whole neighborhood. They put Grandfather onto a stretcher and, sirens still blaring, took him to the hospital. Moments later, a doctor with a haggard face said coldly: "He's been dead for several hours."

Then my parents hired a funeral home to pick up the body and prepare it for burial.

The visitation was short and simple. They placed the coffin, which was open and revealed the motionless body, in a small, dimly lit room. Grandfather looked like he had gained weight since his death; his face was a little fuller, and he was smiling. A couple we know came by to express their condolences. Both of them looked curiously at the body for a moment. The woman wiped away a tear, the man scratched his bald head, and then they left. The truth is that no one else came. Our few friends are working people who spend their evenings doing extra jobs. That's the only way they can survive in this country, where life is expensive. But to tell the truth, sometimes it's like people fall in love with working, and they work like dogs even when they don't have to. That's how this nation was built, by hard work. I myself, even though I'm in school, have to work nights with my father cleaning offices in order to help with our household expenses.

Grandfather was a solitary man with few friends. One of his favorite sayings was that "You're better off alone than in the company of fools."

My parents and I sat silently in the funeral home, meditating and dozing in that room occupied by three living beings and one dead man, waiting for someone else to come to express their sympathies, but no one else came.

There was another visitation in the next room, but the atmosphere there was different, as if those in attendance were happy about the fate of the deceased. We could hear someone singing, and then a woman sobbing loudly. A man said a few words to honor the departed one. Then there was more singing; it combined with the crying to form a noisy din. The funeral home director approached my parents: "Please excuse the noise, but that's how these people have chosen to say goodbye to their loved one. I don't impose restrictions on anyone. Everyone should say farewell as they see fit."

"It sounds more like a party than a funeral," said my father, more surprised than upset.

"That's nothing," said the director. "Just yesterday there was a funeral that resembled a street dance. They brought guitars and drums . . . the walls reverberated to the rhythm of what sounded like a conga drum contest. The police came and asked me if I had turned the place into a nightclub. Just imagine!"

Loud screams and wailing were heard, and the director looked worried and as he was turning to leave, he told my father, "I hope you're pleased with the appearance of your loved one."

"He looks like he gained weight," said my mother.

"The poor man was so thin, he looked like a skeleton. I felt so bad, I filled him in a little," said the director. "Now he looks like a healthy dead man."

This struck me somewhat funny, but I tried to conceal my amusement for fear that my parents would accuse me of disrespecting Grandfather. But I knew that Grandfather would understand my reaction, because he was quite a funny man, a very funny man, in fact, who enjoyed finding the humor in things. He always loved sayings and expressions because, he said, they reflected people's creativity and sense of humor. Grandfather was a great talker too, something I learned from him, or rather something he forced me to learn, since from the moment he set foot in the U.S., he noticed that my Spanish was bad, very bad.

"You spoke better when you were six years old, and now that you're a teenager, you speak half Spanish and half English," he had told me.

I was embarrassed, but he told me not to worry. He got the idea in his head that he would teach me to speak and write Spanish correctly, in exchange for my teaching him English. We made a gentlemen's agreement and taught each other. I think I got the better end of the deal, because he took his teaching very seriously. And since good teachers are bad students, I was never able to teach him much. I learned so many things from Grandfather.

We were only at the funeral home for an hour. There wasn't time for anything more, my father said, because we had to get back to work.

The next day we buried Grandfather without much ceremony, in a city cemetery. Then my parents went back to work, and I went back to school. In other words, we said goodbye to Grandfather exactly the way everything is done in this country, quickly and simply.

I wondered what Grandfather would say now about the way his wake and funeral were conducted. I thought about this because I remembered that, just a few days before he died, he had told me about his grandfather's wake, which sounded more like a party to me.

"Over there, people do things enthusiastically, even burying the dead," he said, as if moved by a premonition. "Not like here, where they do everything so coldly."

ೞ  ೞ  ೞ

I was surprised to hear this, but Grandfather was right.

# 2

Grandfather's death had taken us by surprise. It all happened so unexpectedly that we didn't even have time to stop and think or to do things as he would have wished.

"Sergio, I want to die in my own country," I remember he used to say. "But if by a twist of fate I die here, please bury me in El Salvador."

That was his greatest desire. But it hadn't happened that way.

"He was always going to go back to his country, but for one reason or another, time passed and he never did," said my father.

"He was only coming to visit us for two weeks," Mom agreed. "But we got him a job and he stayed."

"He got so fond of you," said Dad. "And since you were his only grandson, you were like his favorite child."

"You and he were so much alike," said my mother. "He saw something of his own youth in you. And two, three, five years passed, and he never went back. Maybe because he didn't have many friends left back there either. Many of his friends and relatives died while he was here. Whenever he heard that someone had died, he'd say that soon his turn would come, and that therefore he should go back. But he never did."

"We started putting down roots in this country," my father commented, "and ended up staying, even if we didn't want to. After all, we were just coming here to work for a while, make a little money, and go back home and open a business. But now we've been here for many years, we've grown accustomed to this life, and it's not so easy to go back."

"It's not just a matter of packing one's bags and going," Mom added.

That's so true. I came to this country when I was six years old. Now that I'm sixteen, I'm used to this place and I don't know if I can go back to my home country.

# 3

I imagined that Grandfather's homeland was wonderful, because he always told me splendid things that seemed like fantasies. He would talk about the place with such passion that sometimes I thought he was exaggerating.

He saved all the money he made. He dreamed of someday building a house by the sea.

"I don't want a palace," he would say, "just a simple little house on the shore so that I can see the ocean every day before I die."

I don't know what ever happened to that house. The truth is that Grandfather died in the darkness of a room in the middle of the city of Los Angeles, not in the light of a beach in his beloved homeland.

"Someday you must see that magical land," Grandfather would say, showing me postcards and photographs.

I never understood why he didn't go back. I used to tell him: "Grandfather, if you want so badly to be there, why don't you go back, even just to visit for a few weeks?"

He always said he'd go soon, but they were empty words. Finally, one day, because we insisted so much, he went. But two weeks later he was back. He seemed to have aged, as if the trip had not been as good for him as we had hoped. A few days later, he confessed something very sad to me: "I want to go back home, but all my family has died, including your grandmother. You're the only close family I have left."

Then I realized that Grandfather didn't go back because he didn't want to feel alone. From then on I didn't push him. We became close friends. He would tell me experiences of his life in his homeland, and I'd tell him the problems I had at school and other things about my life.

Sometimes on Sundays we went fishing. We'd get up early and get our poles, hooks, bait, and lunch ready. We'd go to Echo Park Lake, rent a boat, load it, and row to the places where the fish were jumping. We'd stay all day.

Grandfather was a crafty fisherman. He knew what bait to use for each kind of fish. We'd make bets as to who'd catch the most fish, and he always won. Sometimes he let me win, though, just so I wouldn't lose interest. He knew that I realized what he was doing, but we were good friends, and good friends understand each other.

It's hard to make good friends in this country. Everyone's always very busy with something, and people don't take time to cultivate friendships. My father, for example, is always busy. We've never gone fishing. Whenever he and I do go out alone together, we're overcome by a profound silence, as if we had nothing to say. But I know we do have a lot to talk about, because he's my father and I'm his son. I wish he'd tell me about our ancestors and the culture of the land where we were born, but he never has time because he's always working.

That's why Grandfather and I became such good friends. I'd keep him company even when I might have preferred to go hang out with my classmates. Grandfather fascinated me, maybe because, after all, we were family.

Sometimes I think that when I get old, I'm going to be just like him. And I know that then Grandfather will be very proud of me.

The fact that Grandfather always wanted to return to his country, even just to be buried, worried me. Whenever I mentioned this to my parents, they always changed the subject, choosing to talk about things they considered more important.

"He's at peace in that cemetery," my father would say.

"But he always wanted to be buried in his homeland," I would respond.

"Bah, once you're buried, the land is one and the same," Mom would conclude.

It seemed I would never be able to convince them of our duty to fulfill Grandfather's wishes, which to me were sacred. I felt that if I could not help him return to his homeland while he was alive, now that he was dead I had to do something. The question was: What to do? It was obvious that my parents didn't care. I was the only one in the family who thought about it. Maybe Grandfather was thinking about it, too . . . from the grave.

# 4

I decided to talk to Mrs. Berenson, the school counselor, a friendly woman I trusted.

The counselor listened to my story patiently, then said, "I can see you loved your grandfather very much."

"Yes, sometimes I think I loved and admired him more than my parents."

My comments didn't surprise her. "I understand you because I too loved my grandparents very much. I know your parents and they're fine people."

"I know they are," I said. "But I feel they're too concerned about money. They work too much, to buy so many things they don't need."

"That's understandable especially for immigrants who were very poor back home. They come here and are dazzled by the abundance and the ease with which material things are acquired here."

"My grandfather liked to say that someone who has nothing and suddenly has too much can end up going crazy."

"Your grandfather was very wise," Mrs. Berenson said, smiling.

"Wise and funny."

I asked her if she had any idea of how to solve my problem.

"It's not easy," she said, "and, besides, it would cost a lot of money to send him home."

"But this is the land of money."

"Maybe so. But it's still hard to get it. Money doesn't grow on trees here, as they believe in other parts of the world. Anyway, I'll find out what procedures have to be followed and how much it would cost to send your grandfather's body back to his country. I'll let you know as soon as I have the information. You can go back to class now."

"I'll really appreciate anything you can do."

"Don't worry, that's what I'm here for. You can count on me."

"Thank you."

Mrs. Berenson's gaze, and her smile, held a shadow of sadness, perhaps nostalgia for something lost or longed for. What was the reason for her sadness? Maybe it was nothing, just my imagination. That was what Grandfather used to tell me sometimes, that I had a lot of imagination, and not to waste that gift from God.

Grandfather gave me a lot of advice. And now that he was dead, I missed him so much. No one could ever take his place. When I think about him, I feel so sad and lonely, but I also feel a strange joy, and that comforts me.

Grandfather used to say that neglect was what pushed many young people in this country to drugs and violence. He always advised me to occupy my mind with something positive. "Idle hands are the devil's workshop," he used to say.

He told me that so many times that it became etched in my mind. I would never do anything bad to anyone, because that would be to insult Grandfather's memory.

"Getting into trouble and vices is the easy way," he'd say. And I would reply that he was right, because it was very easy to get into trouble. On the streets there were drugs, gangs, and weapons. There were also girls who just wanted to have a good time and didn't care if they got pregnant when they were only fifteen or sixteen years old, because they didn't think about the future. Grandfather and I used to talk about all these things.

# 5

**I** was a student at Belmont High, which was located just about a mile from the tall skyscrapers of downtown Los Angeles. It was built in 1923, and it truly amazed me that more than 4,500 students attended school in such an old building.

My school wasn't bad looking; there were others that were worse. It had a generally clean appearance. It wasn't elegant, but it wasn't falling down either. Maybe for people who had never been inside the building the school didn't look so good, but to me it was like home. People said Belmont High didn't have such a good reputation, because of its location, but when you got to know it, you realized it was a good school. To me, Belmont represented the past and the present. The first building, or what was left of it, what they called the West Wing, was the past. The present was represented by more recently constructed portions of the school, such as the main building and the North Wing. All these structures told the school's story. The walls were always full of graffiti, but you learned to live with that and tolerate it . . . what else could you do?

My school was a true melting pot. Most of the students were Latino, Chinese, Korean, African-American, and Filipino. The school offered programs that helped young immigrants prepare for life and become integrated into American culture. Although most of the students were members of ethnic minority groups, there was harmony

among them, a harmony which helped resolve the conflicts that sometimes arose.

The school bathrooms were always dirty and the toi-
lets rarely worked. They smelled bad. They never had toi-
let paper, soap or paper towels. The walls were full of
graffiti.

The classrooms weren't large enough for so many students. They always felt crowded. The paint on the walls was
peeling and the blackboards were permanently dirty—but I
learned a lot in those classrooms. I learned that the world
was enormous, that all human beings were intelligent, and
that each of us had the potential to do great things in life.

I never went to the cafeteria because it was always so
crowded, but my friends said the food wasn't bad, and the
servers were nice. It looked to me like an elementary
school cafeteria. Most of the students just went in and
picked up their food. I always took my own lunch because
the lines in the cafeteria were too long.

I rarely felt in danger at school. Sometimes I felt afraid
to go to school because of the many conflicts in the world,
thinking that a terrorist might come and set off a bomb at
school. But really, I felt safe because I always had friends
around me. Also, there were security guards and cameras at
the main entrance that kept track of anyone going in or out.
Some girls said they felt scared when they were alone in the
third- or fourth-floor bathrooms, but the number of police
officers had increased and they had hired more security per-
sonnel, so I never felt threatened. Sometimes I worried that
gang members might start shooting each other at school,
but fortunately nothing like that ever happened.

# 6

As usual, my parents and I got home around midnight. We were all very tired. There was a lot of work that night. We had to thoroughly clean every office in the building, since they had complained that we weren't doing a good job and we were in danger of losing the contract. Together, my mother, father, and I cleaned a whole office building. It was too much work for three people, but my parents refused to get help because they didn't want to share the money, which they sometimes spent on unnecessary things. My mother always complained of a backache and my father of constant weariness.

One reason they worked so much was that they wanted to buy a house in their home country, where they planned to live in their old age. To me this seemed absurd. I felt it would be better to invest their money and buy a house here. They didn't see it that way, and this was one of the points of contention between my parents and me.

The night job kept me from getting my schoolwork done. As a result, my teachers considered me a mediocre student—according to Grandfather, however, I was very intelligent and had a great imagination.

The school had called my parents several times to discuss my bad grades and see what they could do to help me improve. But since my parents never went to the appointments, the school finally stopped calling. The teachers probably thought that if my parents didn't cooperate, there was nothing more the school could do.

At times, I was so tired that I fell asleep in class and the other students made fun of me. But I knew I wasn't as bad a student as they all thought. I was sure of this because Grandfather had told me so many times.

Before going to bed that night, I decided to ask my parents if they had thought about Grandfather.

"Let him rest in peace," Dad said. "The old man is dead and buried, and I'll bet he's comfortable there, six feet under."

"I don't think so," I ventured, "because he wanted to be buried in his homeland."

"Come on, son, forget about that," Mom urged. "You'd better think about your schoolwork. Your grades are lower than usual. The school has called me three times. I'll have to miss work for a couple of hours just to go hear your teacher complain."

I wanted to tell her my low grades were due to the simple fact that I didn't have enough time to do my homework, because I had to work every night. But they knew that full well, so I decided instead to persist with the subject of Grandfather.

"I think Grandfather would rest in peace if we sent his body to his homeland."

Dad countered, "I'm the one who needs to rest in peace tonight! I'm so tired I could drop. And I have to get up early to go to work. Get to bed, because you have to get up early for school."

Then Mom added: "Besides, we already spent a lot of money on the burial. We don't have more to spend on exhuming the body and paying to ship it and bury it again. We're poor. We don't have money to waste."

"Exactly," my father agreed. "Only the rich could afford the luxury of burying their dead twice."

I went to bed convinced that my parents were determined not to spend another cent on Grandfather. I would have to be the one responsible for returning him to his country. I had made that promise to him when he was alive. I had to keep my word of honor—honor that Grandfather had instilled in me.

# 7

The next day I felt more tired than usual and, without meaning to, I fell asleep with my head on my desk. The teacher woke me abruptly and angrily asked for my homework. I said I hadn't done it.

The other students laughed loudly, further irritating the teacher, who ordered me to leave the room.

He took me to Detention and told the supervisor, "Here's another lazy one," then left.

"Come in," she said. "Take a seat and do your homework quietly." Then she closed the door behind me.

There were two other students in the detention room: a gang member and a girl. The girl was reading. The gang member was pacing the room like a caged animal. The door opened again and Silvia, a classmate of mine, came in.

"They gave me detention again!" she said. "Can I help it that I don't have time to do my homework?"

"I got detention too," said the other girl.

"What for?"

"The same thing."

"Why don't you have time to do your homework?" Silvia asked her.

"I work evenings at a restaurant, and when I get home, all I want to do is sleep, but I have to get up early in the morning to make tortillas."

"Make tortillas?"

"My father eats tortillas every day. And he wants them fresh. So I have to make them for him in the morning."

The gang member was still pacing the room, silently watching the girls. I was sitting at a desk a little ways from them.

"I have to take care of my little brothers and sisters, do the cooking, the cleaning, and the laundry," said Silvia. "The kids go to bed late, and I have to wait for my dad to get home from work and serve him his dinner."

"With all the work I have to do, I don't even have time to think about my homework," said the girl.

"Have you explained that to the teacher?" Silvia asked her.

"I tried once, but she didn't believe me. She said I was lazy and a liar."

"Why do you have to work? Don't your parents make enough to support the family?" I asked the girl.

"I have to help with living expenses, because my parents' salaries aren't enough," she replied. "They don't have good jobs because they don't have legal residency documents. So we're always short of money."

"Money, money, money!" said the gang member. "Everybody goes crazy over money."

Silvia asked me, "What happened to you? Did you fall asleep again?"

"Yes, and I didn't do my homework. . . . After cleaning offices and getting home at midnight, I'm too tired to do my school work."

"Why does your family work so much?" the girl asked me.

"Because my parents took on the job of cleaning a

whole office building all by ourselves. My parents don't hire anyone to help us because they want all the money for themselves."

"I don't do homework 'cause it's useless garbage," said the gang banger.

"But we all gotta," said Silvia. "If we don't, we'll never get ahead."

"None o' the stuff they teach is interesting," added the gang banger.

"What's interesting?"

"Like who I am, what we're doing here in this country . . ."

"That would be good," I said, "because our parents don't have time to explain that to us, or don't want to listen to us."

"We should study the history of our people."

"Me, for example, I don't even know where I'm from," I said. I don't know if I'm from here or there, if I'm Latino or gringo."

"Hey, my gang is my family and my country."

"A gang's a deadend," said the girl. "You in a gang, they can deport you. . . . See how you like that!"

"I'd really like to study, but what I don't have is time," said Silvia.

"I don't either," said the girl. "I come to school so tired that I fall asleep in class."

"So, why'd you get sent to detention?" I asked the gang banger.

"'Cause I don't study, man, why else?"

"Why don't you study?"

"'Cause I don't feel like it! Nobody gonna tell me

what to do. I'm no little kid. They always telling me, 'Do this, do that, dress like this, don't walk like that, talk like this, do this, don't do that.' They think I'm stupid!"

"And you, why do you have to do all the work at home?" the girl asked Silvia. "Don't you have a mother?"

"I'm like the mother at my house," said Silvia.

"What do you mean? Why?"

"Hey, what's your problem? Chill," said the banger. "She got a right to her privacy. You too nosey."

"No, it's okay," said Silvia.

"Hey, you're life's your business. You don't have to tell nobody nothin'."

"I don't mind talking about my life," said Silvia. "Anyway, nobody ever asks me anything. Nobody cares about my life."

"What happened to your mother? Did she die?" asked the girl.

"Hey, quit bugging her!"

"Take it easy, please," I said to the gang banger. "If Silvia wants to talk, it's her business. Nobody's forcing her."

"What happened is that . . . my mother went off with another man . . ." said Silvia. "And now I take care of my younger brothers and sisters and do all the housework . . ."

"Your mother fell in love with another man? Wow, that's awful," I said.

"You don't have to keep talking about it if you don't want to," said the girl. "That's private . . ."

"Why she do that?" asked the gang banger.

"Because she had to," said Silvia.

"What you mean, she had to?" asked the girl.

"To become a legal resident."

"The damn green card!" said the gang banger. "What won't people do to get it!"

"Why not?" I said. "With that card you can live here with no problems, get a good job, buy a house, raise a family, all without being bothered by Immigration."

"My dad has a friend who's legal and is divorced," said Silvia. "After a lot of sacrifice, Dad paid him five thousand dollars to marry my mother so she could get her papers. When she gets them she's supposed to divorce the guy and marry my father again so that all of us can get our green cards."

"Then your mother had to divorce your father before she could marry his friend, right?"

"My mother and father were never legally married in our country."

"Whew, is that complicated," I said.

"But getting married just to get a green card is against the law," said the girl. "If they get caught, you'll all be deported."

"That's why—so it would look normal and Immigration wouldn't suspect anything—my mother moved in with my father's friend until she gets her legal papers."

"How long do they have to live like that?"

"Six more months."

"So it'll all be over soon."

"But it's gotten complicated," said Silvia. "It turns out that my dad's friend gets drunk and rapes my mother. . . . The man says he has the right to do whatever he feels like with my mother because they're legally married. . . ."

"What a—" I said.

"My God!" the girl exclaimed.

"Damn him!" shouted the gang banger.

Silvia bowed her head and fell silent. The girl and I went over to her. The girl stroked her hair in a gesture of understanding and consolation.

Silvia raised her head, crying. "My father wants to kill his friend! But he can't do anything to him because then none of us will get our green cards."

At that moment the bell rang. The supervisor opened the door and came in. "You can go now," she said. "Remember, do your homework, or you'll get detention again."

She stood in the center of the room as we left and said, as if to herself, "I can't understand why these kids don't do their homework. They're so lazy!"

# 8

A few days later I talked to the counselor again. The sadness in her eyes and her smile had not disappeared.

"Without your parents' permission and financial support, we can't do anything," Mrs. Berenson said. "It all depends on them."

"Maybe you can convince them, and make them understand that it's our duty to obey the wishes of the dead."

"If you, their own son, haven't been able to change their minds, I doubt I'll have a chance. But I think there's someone who can convince them."

"Who?"

"Your parish priest."

"I don't think so."

"Why not?" she asked.

"Because we hardly ever go to church."

"That doesn't matter. He's a spiritual leader. Everyone listens to his advice. I'll make an appointment with him so that he can help me."

The next day we went to see the priest. The counselor introduced me.

"I've never seen you around here, son," said Father Michael, looking at me very seriously. "Do you come to Mass on Sundays?"

"No, Father."

"Doesn't your family believe in God?"

"Yes, but in our own way."

"What do you mean?"

"My mother, especially, is always asking for God's help, and asking for favors and blessings."

"That's not believing in God. That's taking advantage of His kindness and patience. How can people ask God to take care of them and bless them, when they don't even visit His house?" Father Michael asked sternly.

"My parents say God's goodness is great, and that He forgives our sins even if we don't have time to go to Mass."

"But it's also necessary to give Him an offering, dedicate some time to Him," the priest insisted.

"But my parents work almost every Sunday."

"Sunday is the Lord's day. They can come to Mass other days," said Father Michael, exasperated. "But anyway, how can I help you today?"

The counselor explained my dilemma in detail.

The priest listened attentively, and then said: "One mustn't play with the remains of the dead. Once they've been buried, they should rest in peace. This is what the will of God and the Church dictate."

"But Grandfather's wish, his will, was to rest in peace in his own land."

"Do you have a document signed by him establishing that this was his desire?"

"No, Father," I replied, disheartened.

"Then there's nothing that can be done. I'm sorry."

The counselor thanked the priest for the time he had

devoted to our visit, and we said goodbye. Before we left, he stopped me and said, more gently, "Tell your parents to be good Christians and come to church, that God is waiting for them."

"Yes, Father."

The priest seemed somewhat perplexed, perhaps because the community no longer attended church in large numbers. My own parents failed to attend Sunday Mass, devoting their time instead to things they couldn't do during the week, like grocery shopping, housecleaning, laundry, and, once in a while, a family conversation. We didn't even have time to rest. I don't remember ever taking a vacation with my family. All my family did was work, something Grandfather always criticized.

# 9

At Belmont High, there were boys with shaved heads who belonged to gangs, but they wouldn't hurt you if you didn't bother them. There were less and less of them all the time. The girls wore dark makeup, the guys dark shirts, wide pants, and expensive brand-name jackets. They didn't go looking for trouble. Grandfather always said that, deep down, most of them just wanted to be different, and wanting to be different from the rest is neither a sin nor a crime. Grandfather also said that such behavior must be used in a positive way, in order to move forward. He didn't defend gangs, but said that some of the reasons for their existence were poverty and lack of education.

Some of my teachers were a real pain; others were lunatics or just hard-nosed. Some didn't know how to teach. I think some of them saw teaching as just another job. But in general, my teachers were good, and I know they wanted me to reach my potential. And some of them were great. There was one teacher who was very popular because he always made us feel comfortable and made us believe we could do great things. He always added good humor to the class and, even when he was angry, he could control his temper. He understood our problems and helped us solve them. Above all, he treated us kindly.

Every teacher at Belmont was different. Some empha-
sized our culture and made us feel proud of our roots, con-
vincing us that we should not feel inferior because we
came from another culture and spoke a different language.

Teachers like that made me want to become a teacher
some day.

Our old Belmont school was supposed to move into a
new, modern building, which was under construction not
very far from the current location. Everything was going
along fine, and the teachers and students were excited
because we were finally going to have a new building with
large classrooms, new bathrooms, a big cafeteria, and
modern sports facilities. But one day it was announced
that the plans were canceled, that they would not finish
the building. They had discovered that the ground there
was contaminated, an ecological disaster, the former site
of a chemical dump. Belmont High would stay right
where it was, in the old building.

Every day I looked at the "new" building and felt kind
of sad. I heard the Science teachers say that the building
could be finished and classes held there with no health
risk to the students. Others said that the county didn't
want to invest any more money to finish the building
because they were afraid the students would become ill
there. All this created a huge controversy, but many students and parents did not seem interested in expressing an
opinion about it. I was one of the few students who attended the couple of after-school meetings that were held
about this issue. I was sure that if we students didn't show
any interest, no one else would care if the bathrooms at
the old school were dilapidated and foul-smelling, the

cafeteria too small for the more than 4,500 students, and the fact that between classes it was impossible to walk down the halls due to the huge numbers of students. Some of my classmates believed that all this was due to political corruption. Others said that the rich people didn't want to see poor students get ahead. On the other hand, many students feared that if we moved into the new building, the contamination would affect us physically and mentally to the point of deforming our bodies, that we could grow an extra arm. What was the real reason? We weren't sure.

# 10

Grandfather and I talked about things that I didn't talk about with anyone else, not even my parents, such as the strange feeling I'd had ever since I came to this country. I suspected it was similar to the feelings experienced by thousands of young people like me, who came to this country very young or were born here to immigrant parents.

"I feel strange. I don't know if I'm from here or from there," I confessed to Grandfather one day.

"I understand, Sergio. It's just that you haven't completely adapted to this society, even though you've lived here for years. It's a matter of identity, because you don't know if you're from this country or your parents' country. . . . Besides, what does our native land mean to a boy like you, who came to the U.S. when you were only six and only vaguely remember your birthplace?"

"My father has nothing but bad things to say about the old country. He says he was treated very badly and never given the opportunity to get ahead," I said. "But my mother remembers it fondly, in spite of everything."

"For me, my homeland is my umbilical cord," said Grandfather. "But I also understand that for many young people like you, the homeland is no longer yours. And sometimes your adoptive home doesn't feel enough like home either."

"So then, which one is my country, Grandfather?"

"Your country, Sergio, is a problem."

"But what's the solution to this problem? Because as long as I don't decide, I feel left out, like I don't belong to this land even though I live here."

"Time is the only solution. Time heals everything. As you can see, I'm in a situation similar to yours. I'm not from this country, nor can I return to my home, because everything has changed. The place I come from exists only in my memory. The people and customs have all changed."

"And how long does it take to get used to this?" I asked.

"Sometimes a couple of years. Sometimes a lifetime. But don't worry, just take things as they come. The secret is to be flexible and try to adapt to any situation. Kind of like the chameleon that changes its color according to the environment."

"In my case, sometimes I want to be like my parents, retain their culture, but then I realize that the rest of the world is different. And when I try to make friends with other kids who I think are in situations like mine, the last thing they want is to be like their parents. They want to adapt to the culture of this country any way they can, and be like everybody else. They forget their Latino roots and don't speak Spanish. Then I think that I'm the problem because I'm trying to go against the grain."

"There's nothing bad about wanting to be what you want to be," Grandfather assured me, "about wanting to know where you come from and learn about your roots and your ancestors."

"But what culture do I belong to? What is my identity?" I insisted.

"For starters, you shouldn't feel bad about not fitting in completely in the United States. You're part of a new identity that is the product of two cultures: your parents' culture and the culture of this country. These two form a third culture, to which you belong: a culture made up of two different cultures and languages. You are what they call here bicultural and bilingual. This is something very positive that gives you a lot of personal advantages. You should be proud of who you are."

"Could that be why at school they call me Fifty-Fifty?"

Grandfather laughed heartily, causing me to do the same, and the two of us had a great laugh together.

"What a clever nickname. So you're half from there and half from here, nothing more and nothing less."

Grandfather was right, the two of us were in similar situations. Maybe that's why we understood each other so well. Sometimes my parents were even slightly envious of our long conversations in Grandfather's room. My mother would call down to us, "Quit talking so much! Come out of that room. You're not rats!"

# 11

When I was little, my mother took care of me while she was working in rich people's houses in El Salvador. I would follow her with my short steps through all the rooms as she did the cleaning. She would finish before supper, and even though she was tired and hungry by then, we would wait for her employer and his family to have dinner. Only after they had finished could we eat the leftovers. Sometimes they had long conversations, and the servants had to wait in the kitchen until they finished. Then the maids would remove the dishes from the table, and divide the leftovers among us. My mother always gave me a bone to keep me busy licking it. Now that I'm older, I hate bones. As far as I'm concerned, they're for dogs.

I vaguely remember that in the mansion where my mother worked, there was someone who embraced her and took her off to the bedroom while I was busy playing. I always wanted to ask my mother who that person was, but I didn't have the kind of relationship with her that would allow me to do that. I was afraid she'd find the question out of line and be shocked that I had remembered all that. I remember that and much more: her hardships, her exhaustion, the mistreatment she received from the employers. Grandfather said childhood memories were the strongest and lasted throughout our lives.

"Surely that was your father," Grandfather told me once when I told him what I remembered. "He was a servant at the house where your mother worked. Later, they left that job and came to live with me. Life was hard for them. Several years later, with great sacrifice, they managed to get together enough money to pay a smuggler, who brought them to this country when you were little."

"I remember some of that too," I told him. "And that memory is even more unpleasant."

"You're right. I'm familiar with the details of the trip. It sure wasn't easy."

"In this country my mother does the same thing: she cleans houses for the wealthy. And my father is a laborer. So, as for work, things have changed very little for them."

"On the contrary," said Grandfather, "I would say that things have changed a lot, because back home they worked very hard and earned very little. Here, they work just as hard but are paid ten times more. Besides, over here the jobs aren't as demeaning as they are back home."

# 12

My neighborhood was very lively. There was always plenty of action and an atmosphere similar to that of Belmont High, with Latino immigrants from different countries. The neighborhood was fun, noisy, and crowded, but somewhat dirty, made up of houses and small buildings in an area that some people called a ghetto. It was inhabited by good, hardworking people. There were mothers walking with their children, kids playing and having good clean fun. But there were also gang members, and you never knew what to expect from them.

There was lots of graffiti on the walls in the neighborhood. During the day, women sold food, clothing, and snow cones on the sidewalks. There was lots of movement and noise outside. But at night it became a nightmare, because there were young men with guns wandering the streets, and you never knew if someone was going to get shot.

There was vandalism on my street, and people said there was some drug-trafficking too. When I got home from school, I didn't look out the window much, because I had to make good use of the time I had to do some homework. I never got it all done, though, because of working nights with my parents. There was less violence in the neighborhood after a police unit had been transferred to my street. People felt safer with police cars going by all the time.

My parents and I lived quite close to the school. Belmont was on Loma and I lived two blocks over, on Union. Most of the people who lived there left for work early in the morning.

When we left home every morning, my parents would walk with me to the school. From there, they continued down to Beverly Boulevard to catch the bus that took them to their job in the home of a rich family in Beverly Hills. My mother did the cleaning and my father took care of the garden and home repairs.

At school I had quite a few friends, many of them from different ethnic backgrounds. Interestingly, they were all like me: funny and sincere. One of my friends cared a lot about how she looked and was always buying clothes. Another was always trying to forget her ex. A third one, in contrast, was looking for a boyfriend and was still very much in love with her ex. All my female friends were sweet and affectionate; some were just plain crazy. All my friends were good people; we were always willing to help each other in any way. If I had trouble in a subject at school, they helped me understand it. These friendships were very important to me. Grandfather always agreed with me on that. He said it was better to have friends than to have money.

My best friend Luis always listened to me and made me feel intelligent and special. Other than Grandfather, he was the only person I could confide in, because he was trustworthy, warm, and kind. He made me laugh when I was sad and was always great to talk to. Luis was like the brother I never had. We had met in seventh grade. His family was from Guatemala. He had come to this country when he was small, like I did. He was friendly to everyone and could be a little crazy sometimes. I could always count on his support when I needed it most. He helped me understand that we had to put a lot of effort into our schoolwork in order to prepare for life. He considered me his best friend, too, because I'd been with him in difficult situations and always supported him, like when he got involved in drugs and felt so alone and trapped by his addiction. Everyone else turned their backs on him. When he finally recovered, he told me that my friendship and understanding had helped him give up drugs. Grandfather met him and said he seemed like a good kid.

When Luis and I talked, he always spoke English, even when I spoke Spanish to him. He did the same with his parents, although it was harder for them to understand him because they didn't speak English very well. I didn't have any trouble understanding him, since I knew both languages.

People looked at us strangely when they heard us talking to each other because, although I understood English, I spoke only Spanish to Luis, and although Luis understood Spanish, he spoke only English to me. Our conversations were like a language competition, but we still understood each other perfectly.

When Luis met Grandfather, I had to interpret for them. Luis understood everything Grandfather was saying to him in Spanish, but spoke to him in English, and so that Grandfather wouldn't be lost, I had to translate. It was a very complicated conversation, because there came a time when none of us was sure if we really understood what the others were saying. In the end, we realized that the whole thing was funny and we all ended up having a good laugh.

# 13

The counselor came to my classroom and asked me to stop by her office that afternoon. I figured she was going to update me on the obstacles we still faced, and the new ones that came up every day, for returning Grandfather to his land. I had fulfilled my part of the agreement she and I had made. I had saved some money. I was working weekends washing cars, and I was also saving the money my mother gave me for school. I had looked through Grandfather's papers and given the counselor the names and addresses of some people he knew in his country.

When I arrived at her office, the counselor was busy with several students who were in trouble. Among them was a known gang member. I wondered what he had done this time. The counselor was trying to mediate between the principal, who wanted to expel the boy, and the boy's parents, who were begging the principal to forgive him. The boy sat silently; he didn't seem to care what they did with him.

There was also a pregnant girl, barely fifteen years old. She was crying and complaining of abuse from her parents and from classmates, who considered her a fool for getting pregnant without realizing the consequences. She wasn't sure who the father of the child was. She confessed that she regretted having gotten pregnant and was willing to place the baby with an adoption agency.

The third boy had been in a fight. His face was bruised, his clothes dirty and his shirt torn. He was being escorted by one of the school guards.

The counselor interrupted her meeting to tell me she would be busy all afternoon and that I should come back the next day. I felt a dark foreboding that she didn't have good news, and I went home somewhat downhearted.

The next afternoon, the counselor was talking to a boy who was always in trouble for not doing his homework. I felt kind of sorry for him, because I had been in that situation many times. The difference was that he didn't do his homework because he didn't feel like it. In my case, I didn't have time to do it.

The boy left and Mrs. Berenson stood up to greet me. She looked tired and nervous, as usual, but this time a big smile lit up her face.

"I have good news," she said.

Those words surprised me.

"You do?"

"Yes. I got in touch with the Salvadoran embassy, and they told me what we have to do to send his body back."

"But who will be there to receive it?"

"One of the names you gave me turned out to be his cousin, your great aunt. I contacted her and she offered to pick up the body and bury it there."

"I've saved some money, but I don't think it's enough . . ."

"You're not going to believe this," she said excitedly, "but your grandfather had saved a lot of money and sent it to his cousin to keep for him. It's enough to pay for the trip!"

"It looks like it's all set, then!"

"Almost. We just need your parents' authorization."

"I think that will be easy now, since it won't cost them a penny."

Suddenly I felt a strong impulse that shook my entire body, and I shouted, "I'm going with Grandfather!"

Mrs. Berenson looked at me strangely, and for a moment it was as though she didn't know what to say.

"You'll get behind in your schoolwork," she finally said.

"That doesn't matter. I'll study hard when I get back."

"You don't know anyone there, Sergio. You came to this country when you were little."

"I'll get to know my great aunt. She's family."

"Who'll pay for your trip?"

"I've saved money."

"Your parents won't let you."

"We'll convince them. I know you'll help."

Seeing my determination, she smiled with an expression of complicity.

"Okay. So far we've managed to overcome the most difficult obstacles. Now we'll try to convince your parents."

# 14

Mrs. Berenson came to my house that weekend. After talking to my parents about school, work, family, and the weather, she got to the point: "Everything has been arranged for Sergio's grandfather to return to his country."

My parents didn't say a word, I don't know if out of surprise at the news or because they felt guilty for not having done anything to help fulfill Grandfather's wishes.

"Now Grandfather's dream will come true," I added, supporting the counselor's words.

My mother was the first to react: "We can't afford it."

"His cousin will pay for everything," said the counselor.

"Everything?"

"Everything."

"As far as I know, she has barely enough money to support herself," my mother objected.

"Grandfather saved everything he made at his job and sent it to her," I said.

"That crafty old fox!" said my father. "He had everything figured out. So many people work hard in order to have a better life; he did it to be buried in his own way."

"And to return to his homeland," I added.

"Who will take care of the arrangements?" my mother asked.

"A funeral home," Mrs. Berenson answered. "They'll prepare the body, take it to the airport, and put it on the plane."

"And who will receive it over there?"

"His cousin has hired a funeral home to receive the body and bury it."

"It looks like everything's all set, then," said my mother.

"Everything," agreed the counselor.

"Well, then, let Grandfather's will be done," said my father.

"So be it," agreed my mother.

The counselor caught my eye to cue me that this was the right time for me to express my wishes.

"I'm going with Grandfather," I said.

"You're crazy!" my father exclaimed.

"What about school" added my mother.

"We need your help at work."

"You don't have any family over there."

"And it's dangerous, especially for a young man like you."

I couldn't think of any arguments to refute those objections. All I could say was, "I want to bury Grandfather in his homeland, to be with him in the final moments, and show him my true love, as he did with me."

"Grandfather is already dead and buried. I hope God doesn't punish us for allowing them to exhume him," my mother said.

"It's his wish. I think he'll be glad to have me go with him to his native land."

"Did he ask you to?" my mother inquired.

"Yes."

My father looked me right in the eye. "Are you sure?"

"I'm sure," I said firmly.

For Grandfather's sake, I had just lied for the first time. I knew he would forgive me, because I had done it out of my love for him, to be close to him, in his homeland, for the last time.

The counselor, trying to help me, spoke up: "He can take along his books and study during the trip, so he won't fall behind."

"And over there I can stay with my aunt until we bury Grandfather."

"I don't see any problem with it," Mrs. Berenson agreed. "Besides, I believe it's important for this boy's emotional state that he accompany his grandfather to his final resting place. It'll be good for him. It will help his self-esteem."

"And Grandfather will be happy," I added.

My parents didn't seem convinced, but in the end they gave in.

"Okay, I'll let you go for a week, but no longer," said my father.

I was so happy that I jumped up and down and hugged the counselor and my parents. That was one of the happiest moments of my life. Grandfather was probably jumping for joy up in heaven.

# 15

Belmont High had a long history and a great tradition. Many of its graduates had become very important people. Belmont was a pleasant place, full of energy, because it was composed of students who might not have been the best in the world, but once we graduated, we made it our own. Despite all of Belmont's problems, I liked it and was very proud of it, the students, the teachers, and my friends.

Some of the teachers complained about parents' lack of involvement in their children's education and their lack of interest in school issues. But I understood that most of the parents couldn't help their children with their homework because they were always working in order to survive and support their families, and in some cases because they didn't even speak English. The parents did not participate in discussions of school-related issues or work toward improving the schools because they were afraid to get involved, since many of them had not yet resolved their immigration status in this country.

In my case, as was certainly the case with most of the students, what I wanted was to be successful in life. Of course, there were stumbling blocks, but in order to overcome them, I would think about my parents and what they had endured to come to this country and give me a better life. That's why I wanted to stay in school and have a career, and make my parents proud. I knew it wouldn't be easy because students like me faced serious obstacles to attaining a better education. Many wanted to go to college but couldn't afford it or didn't have legal documents.

Grandfather always said it wasn't the buildings that made the school, no matter how fancy or ugly they might be, but the teachers and especially the students. In that sense I considered Belmont a great school.

Many people referred to Belmont as "full of Latinos and gangs," which was far from the truth. The existence of gangs didn't mean they controlled the school. Instead of focusing on that, those people should have been taking note of how hard our people were working to live with dignity and get ahead in this country.

"Necessity forces us to get used to the place where we live, however miserable it may be," Grandfather would say as he recalled his homeland and his people. "But the challenge for each of us lies not in scorning it, but in discovering the positive in that place and improving it."

Grandfather always had an opinion about everything and never kept his opinions to himself. And he encouraged me to do the same. Sometimes my parents told me not to heed his advice.

"The old man talks too much," my father had told me. "No one can keep him quiet."

"Back home in his country he got into a lot of trouble because he told everyone the truth right to their face," my mother had agreed.

"One time they put him in jail for criticizing the government," my father revealed to me. "But, despite that, he didn't change."

"But now we're here in the United States," Grandfather had argued. "This is supposed to be a free country, where you can speak your mind. It's every citizen's duty to express his opinions, however good or bad they may be, and to respect the opinions of others."

My parents were right. They had never been able to keep Grandfather quiet; he considered himself a completely free man. And that's why he would always be my hero.

# 16

The long-awaited day of traveling to Grandfather's homeland finally came. My parents took me to the airport and there we met Mrs. Berenson. She had come to make sure that Grandfather's body was delivered to the airline. Through the terminal window, we saw the enormous container that held the coffin being loaded into the cargo compartment of the plane.

When the time came to say goodbye, my parents urged me to take care of myself and come home soon. Then I thanked Mrs. Berenson for having made the trip possible.

"Don't forget to send me a postcard," she reminded me.

I got on the plane, and soon it took off and climbed into the sky. My entire body trembled with excitement. I was so happy that Grandfather and I were flying toward the land he loved so much. It was as if he had planned it all himself and was just pretending to be dead so that together we could fly to that land where he and I were born. I was traveling very comfortably in my seat, and he in his coffin.

The plane was flying through the blue sky above the clouds that looked like mountains of cotton. The trip was long because we had to fly over the southwestern states and the Gulf of Mexico. As we flew over the open waters of the gulf, I was able to read my textbooks and do some homework. However, the emotions of the trip drained me and, after a while, I fell into a deep sleep.

# 17

I had slept about an hour when I was awakened by the alarmed shouts of the passengers. Then I heard the pilot announce, "Ladies and gentlemen, I regret to inform you that the plane is having engine trouble, and we have been unable to determine the cause . . ."

The passengers immediately became terrified and confused.

"We're going down!" someone screamed.

The pilot confirmed it: "Ladies and gentlemen, we're losing altitude fast. Prepare for an emergency landing. Please obey all instructions from your flight attendants. Keep your seatbelts tightly fastened; that is the most important thing."

The atmosphere in the plane, calm only a few minutes earlier, had changed radically. Many of the passengers were hysterical. Several were screaming desperately, while others were praying loudly.

"This can't be happening!" one man cried out. "I was going on vacation and now I'm going to die!"

"We must commend our souls to God!" exclaimed a woman.

The captain was issuing instructions over the loudspeaker. The flight attendants struggled to walk up and down the aisle comforting the passengers, but terror clouded their faces.

"We're all going to drown!" someone screamed.

The plane began to descend more quickly. The captain announced, "Good news, ladies and gentlemen: we still have one working engine that will help us descend over the water . . ."

"My God, we'll drown!" said a panicked woman.

"If the sharks don't devour us!" exclaimed a man.

"I'm afraid!" cried a little boy.

The captain added, "Don't worry: if all goes well, the plane will float like a boat, and we'll be rescued by the Coast Guard. I have experience flying hydroplanes, which will serve us well here . . ."

"What the hell is a hydroplane?" asked a desperate man.

"A plane that floats on water," responded a flight attendant.

The plane was going down quickly, and all the passengers feared the worst. The flight attendants told us what we had to do when the plane hit the water. The seat cushions would be our life preservers. The oxygen masks dropped from the ceiling, and we were told to put them over our noses and mouths.

Meanwhile, the plane was lurching from side to side and making strange noises as it passed through areas of turbulence. I felt a strange sensation in my stomach, like when going downhill on a roller coaster. Several passengers were vomiting and coughing. The inside of the plane, now a scene of complete panic, had heated up and was filled with a strange smell. Through the windows we could see the sea, just the sea.

In my row, the woman in the middle seat fainted. The man next to her was praying quietly, his eyes closed. I

tried to pay attention to everything that was happening in
the plane and the instructions of the pilot and crew members.

"We're approaching the water," the captain's calm
voice announced. "Please check your seatbelts and grasp
the back of the seat in front of you. That way you won't
feel such a strong impact."

The plane descended and slid across the water. Bounc-
ing and bumping along, it gradually slowed down and
finally stopped, floating and rocking like a boat on the
high seas. Some of the passengers applauded happily,
realizing we had survived the landing.

The emergency doors were opened immediately. We
had made it through the initial fright. Miraculously, there
had been no casualties yet. Some passengers were moaning, and several children were crying, but the captain
appeared to have everything under control.

With the help of some passengers who had left the
plane and were standing on the wings, several rafts were
inflated and tossed into the water. We all got on the rafts,
making sure to bring the seat cushions that would function
as life preservers if it became necessary to jump into the
water. Within a short time, everyone had left the plane,
including the captain and the crew.

"The plane is sinking!" someone shouted.

"Goodbye, suitcases!" someone else exclaimed.

Several people laughed nervously.

"As long as we're safe, who cares about the luggage!"

"That's right, our lives are more important."

The captain commented that the belly of the plane had
likely cracked open during the descent; that was how the

water was getting in. Immediately I thought of Grandfather. The poor man would sink with the plane and end up at the bottom of the ocean, which was not at all what he had wanted. He had never even been a sailor. He loved fishing, but I don't think he would have chosen to be buried at sea and have his body devoured by fish.

Suddenly a woman shouted, "The suitcases came out of the plane!"

"That one's mine!" exclaimed a man.

The bags were floating in the water, and several passengers complained that their belongings were going to be ruined.

Suddenly someone asked, "What's that floating over there?" He pointed toward the sinking plane.

I turned to look in the direction the man was pointing. An enormous container was rocking on the waves. I shouted excitedly, "It's my grandfather!"

I jumped into the water and swam toward the huge container, clinging to it with all my strength.

"Hang on tight!" the captain shouted.

"Watch out for sharks!" said a flight attendant.

At that moment a man let out a loud cry of happiness as he saw some boats approaching.

"It's the Coast Guard!" the captain confirmed. "Thank God!"

The Coast Guard rescued us. I had climbed onto the container, which was floating on the water like a sturdy raft. Several men descended from a helicopter and secured the huge box with thick cables; then they raised it into the air and lowered it onto the deck of one of the boats. Grandfather and I were saved!

By then the plane had sunk completely, but no one died in the disaster. The only losses were most of the suitcases and the plane itself.

On board the Coast Guard ships, all the passengers laughed happily at having survived that strange accident that could well have sank us to the bottom of the Gulf of Mexico.

# 18

The Coast Guard ships took us to a port where we were met by television cameras and reporters who wanted to know every detail of the accident. When they found out that I was traveling with a dead man, they fired all kinds of questions at me and were not satisfied until I told them everything about the trip and what it meant to me. A newspaper published a story about the case with the headline "Boy Travels with Grandfather in Coffin. Both Survive Air Disaster."

After a few hours, they put us up in a hotel, and I called my parents from there. Luckily, I found them at home. My mother had seen a television report on the accident and was very worried.

"I'm so glad you called, son. It was such a shock to see you on TV. What a tragedy!"

"Don't worry, Mom, I'm fine. A little shaken up, that's all. But, thank God, we're all safe, including Grandfather," I reassured her.

"Well, he's already dead and can't die again, no matter how many accidents he has."

I wanted to tell my mother that to me Grandfather wasn't dead. During the trip and the accident, I had felt his presence so close to me, as if he were my guardian angel protecting me from all dangers. But I wasn't able to tell her that because she handed the phone to my father who said, "See the problems you've gotten yourself into burying people twice? It's bad luck! But you don't listen! Instead of wasting your time and looking for trouble, you should be home with your parents, helping us at work and studying."

My mother took the phone back and said in a conciliatory tone, "Don't mind your father. He's very glad, as I am, that you're all right. It's just hard for him to tell you that he loves you and misses you a lot."

"I understand," I said.

"And now what?" she asked.

"Tomorrow, we'll continue the trip by plane."

"God willing, there'll be no more problems. Call us when you get to your great aunt's house."

"Yes, Mamá."

"I love you very much. Take care of yourself. Remember that you're my only son."

"I love you very much too, Mamá. You're my only, sweet mother."

My father took the phone. "Son, take care of yourself. Don't forget your parents. We're waiting for you here with open arms." My father finally seemed to feel some emotion. "All our love, son. God bless you."

"Thanks, Dad. I love you very much."

"Goodbye, son," said my mother. "Good luck."

"Goodbye."

# 19

We continued on our way the next day, as if nothing had happened. Three hours later, we landed at our destination with no further complications.

When the door of the plane opened and I went out into the fresh air, my first impression was that I was entering a different world, full of color and fantasy. The climate was pleasant, not too hot and not too cold. A gentle breeze caressed my skin, and I felt my heart enveloped in a joy I had never known. It was as if I were welcomed home after ten years away.

My great aunt turned out to be a cheerful, dynamic, beautiful woman, with a joy for living that made her look very young. She immediately took care of everything. The coffin was taken to the funeral home, where the wake would be held the following day. I accompanied my aunt to her home, a small, modest dwelling that was neat and clean, with a garden and a lemon tree that perfumed the air.

"You can sleep in this room," she told me. "It's the same one where your grandfather stayed the only time he came to visit from the United States. I remember he told me then that he had a great friend over there, and that was the only reason he was going back. Now I realize he was talking about you."

"Yes, more than relatives we were friends."

"That's beautiful. Friendship is one of the most precious gifts in life. True friendship is everything: trust, understanding, warmth, tolerance, love."

"Grandfather used to say that having friends was better than having money."

"He was a kind and eloquent man. You'll see tomorrow how many people come to the wake. A lot of people knew him."

Darkness found us still chatting in the garden.

"There's something I want to tell you before I forget," she said. "From the moment I saw you, it was as if I were looking at your grandfather. . . . Not only do you look like him, but you even have the same aura about you. Do you know what I mean? It's as if you were his reincarnation. And look, I'm not religious or superstitious; I don't even believe in life after death. But it's like you're cut from the same cloth. You even have the same faraway stare."

My aunt inspired so much confidence and trust in me that I told her what I hadn't been able to tell my mother: that I felt Grandfather's presence very strongly, as if he were by my side day and night.

"Maybe the two of you are the same person," she said in her naturally charming way. "You know, I never told your grandfather, but I was always in love with him. He was my secret love."

"While we're on the subject, I want to tell you a secret," I confessed.

"You do? What is it?"

"That Grandfather was in love with you, too. He never told you, since you two were cousins and he was afraid that if you had children, they'd be born with defects."

She let out a laugh, and her whole body seemed to tremble with energy. "Your grandfather had such a sense of humor!"

"The two of you would have made a fabulous couple. You are a beautiful woman, in every sense of the word, just like he described you."

"My goodness," she said with emotion, "you're gallant with women just like your grandfather. You must have a lot of girlfriends in the United States."

"No, not a single one."

Then I added: "That business of girlfriends is really complicated."

"Why do you say that?"

"It's just that in the U.S., lots of immigrant parents want their sons to find girlfriends who have the same customs as in their home country, but the boys want girlfriends who've adapted to U.S. customs."

"And what do you prefer?" she asked.

"I haven't really thought about it."

"That's okay, don't worry, all in due time," she advised.

It was late, and we decided to turn in. I was very tired, but also very amazed by that enchanting place and that woman who, despite her years, had a young spirit and a joy for living.

Before going to bed, my great aunt knocked on the door of my room and said, "I'm so glad you're here. From this moment on, you are my dear grandson. You've made me so happy with your visit."

"Thank you so much, Tía. I'm happy too that I've met you and that I'm here with you in Grandfather's land."

"Remember, it's your land too," she said in a gentle, melodious voice. "You were born near here."

"I was? I didn't know that."

"Tomorrow we'll visit your birthplace. Sweet dreams. Good night."

"Good night."

# 20

I rarely dreamed, perhaps because I had nothing to dream about. But that night I had a very strange dream.

I dreamed that I had become Grandfather. It was as if he were young again.

In my dream, my great aunt was a young girl, beautiful and radiant as a flower, and she was playing innocent children's games with her cousin (that is, Grandfather, but me in the dream).

They grew up, and those childish games turned into love. The two of them fell in love, but their families did not approve of that romance between blood relatives. So one night, without telling anyone, they ran off together to the United States, where they consummated their great love and lived happily ever after.

A rooster's crowing awakened me. I still felt in my body the strange sensation of love and happiness from that dream that Grandfather perhaps had dreamed from his coffin, through me, to finally consummate his secret love, and so that I, for the first time, would experience the happiness of love.

# 21

**M**y aunt took me to see the place where I was born. It was a small house, its paint peeling, inhabited by people who were coming and going, busy with their daily tasks.

"They're descendants of your grandfather," my aunt said.

"They're my relatives?"

"No, I don't think so because they're from a distant generation," she explained.

My aunt took me by the hand and we approached the house. We met a woman my aunt knew.

"How nice to see you" the woman replied. "You haven't been here for a long time."

"I'm happy to see you, too. I'd like you to meet my grandson. He's visiting from the United States."

"Nice to meet you," said the woman.

"Nice to meet you," I said.

My aunt added, "He was born in this house sixteen years ago, so I wanted to show it to him."

"Come in," the woman invited us. "Forgive the mess."

My aunt went in and called to me: "Come on, come in. Look, this is the room where your mother gave birth to you. I remember it very well, because I came to see her the day after you were born. You were a plump, cheerful little baby."

I went into the room. I felt a strange warmth that caused me to recall vague images from my childhood. As I scrutinized the dark, empty interior of the house, I realized how poor my parents had been. Now, I really understood their effort to go to another country to seek a better life.

"Well," said my aunt, "now you've seen it. We'd better get going before it gets too late. We have a very busy day today."

I turned to leave, and as I did, I bumped into a young girl. She smiled, and her face lit up. Her intense gaze caught me so by surprise that I had to struggle to take my eyes off her.

"Well, look who's here," said my aunt. "It's Flor de Ángel. She was born the same day and time as you. You're exactly the same age. When you were little, you used to play together."

I held out my hand. "Nice to meet you."

"The pleasure is mine. What's your name?"

"Sergio."

"Like your grandfather," she said and continued on her way without saying goodbye.

"Let's go," said my aunt.

We left. We took care of all the things we had to do that day. In the evening we went to the funeral home for Grandfather's wake. I was surprised to find that there were quite a few people there already.

"All these people knew your grandfather," my aunt confirmed.

"I never knew he was so popular."

"This is nothing. Wait 'til you see how many more people come later."

We sat down near the coffin. My aunt was right: many people filed past the coffin. They would stop and pray silently, then come over to greet my aunt, who introduced me to all of them. They all said I looked a lot like Grandfather. They told me how much they liked him and expressed their sympathies at his death and the fact that he had died despite having always been so strong and full of life.

This wake was so different from the first one! The one in the U.S. was quick and lonely. This one was full of people and commotion. Several of those who came hadn't seen each other for many years. Greeting each other happily, they exchanged anecdotes about Grandfather.

The hours were passing and people showed no sign of being ready to leave. Flor de Ángel arrived with her family. I shook her soft hand and my legs felt so weak, I had to sit down to keep from falling.

She smiled and asked, "Are you coming to the carnival tomorrow?"

"What carnival?"

"The carnival of the dead," she replied. "I imagine you'll take your grandfather, won't you?"

I had no idea what she was talking about, but I said yes, maybe just out of my desire to see her again. Her smile revealed perfect white teeth. Her tanned face shone brightly with joy. Her dark hair, soft and wavy, invited my touch. She was full of freshness and vitality. Soon she walked away, but I couldn't take my eyes off her.

My aunt came over to me and, in a curious tone, said, "She's pretty, isn't she?"

"Very pretty," I said, unable to hide my admiration for

Flor de Ángel. Even her name sounded delicate and poetic to me, perfect for her.

Then I asked my aunt, "What's the carnival of the dead?"

"It's a traditional festival in which we bid farewell to those who have died recently and remember those who died a long time ago. What a coincidence that the carnival starts tomorrow, on the very day of your grandfather's burial. I've reserved a place in the procession."

This sounded a little strange to me, but when I stopped to think that Grandfather would have wanted it, I decided that it would be a good idea to participate in that tradition. Besides, it would be another opportunity to see Flor de Ángel and talk to her.

# 22

The procession was part of a carnival with music and costumes. Grandfather's friends took turns carrying his coffin, which was transported on a platform with six handgrips, three on each side. They put me right up in front, and I helped carry it, but only for half a block because there were so many who also wanted to have the honor.

There were at least a hundred coffins in the parade, some containing bodies and others empty, carried by families in memory of their loved ones. Surrounding the coffins were individuals dressed in costumes of skeletons and other characters from beyond the grave. They blew on whistles and beat drums. Several bands played loud, lively music. It was a crowded, joyful celebration that bore no resemblance whatsoever to a funeral. Its purpose was to create enough life, noise, and happiness to awaken the dead and show them that they had not been forgotten, that they were remembered with a great deal of happiness.

Someone disguised as a dead person came up to me. When she took off her mask, I saw that it was my aunt. She laughed heartily when she saw that she had frightened me. She hugged me and then put her mask back on and went off into the crowd again in search of more victims.

At that moment Flor de Ángel arrived. She wasn't wearing a costume or disguise—good thing! There was a crowd of people close behind her. I took her by the hand and we stepped aside to allow the group to go past, but a dance troupe swept us up and we got caught in the middle of it. Flor de Ángel started dancing and invited me to do the same. I told her I didn't know how to dance.

"You'll learn now!" she shouted. "It's easy. Just let yourself move to the rhythm of the music."

She said it so sweetly that I ventured to move my feet. "That's it," she said, "just like that."

The procession finally reached the cemetery, and I ran on ahead to find Grandfather's coffin. They had already placed it in the ground. When I reached her side, my aunt invited me to place the first shovelful of dirt into the grave. Then Grandfather's friends and acquaintances each took a turn, until the box was completely covered. Flor de Ángel placed a beautiful bouquet of flowers on the grave. Suddenly I felt tremendous satisfaction. Grandfather finally was buried in his own land. His sacred wish had been fulfilled!

That journey had been the greatest adventure of my life. It had allowed me to discover some of my roots, the customs of my ancestors, and the land of my childhood. I had met a great aunt who loved life and Flor de Ángel, a beautiful flower of my homeland.

With his death, Grandfather had given me the lesson of my life. Yet I still firmly believed that he was not dead, that he lived on in me and in all those he touched on his journey through this world.

Although the dead had been buried, the carnival was still going strong. Flor de Ángel and I walked through the park, enjoyed typical foods and danced to several songs. She was surprised at how easily I learned as I followed her lead.

The carnival hadn't ended, but a new day was dawning as I walked Flor de Ángel home. We said goodbye, and I kissed her soft cheek nervously.

"When are you going back to the United States?" she asked.

I sighed and said, "I don't know. Maybe tomorrow. Maybe never."

"If you go, I'm going with you."

That revelation caught me by surprise and, not knowing what to say, I asked, "And if I stay?"

"I will too."

I couldn't hold back anymore and I kissed her soft lips.

"See you tomorrow."

"It's already tomorrow," she said with a smile.

"See you later, then."

"Don't be long."

"Okay."

She pushed open the door and entered the dark house where she lived, the house where I was born.

I went back to my aunt's house. I was tired after all the events of the previous day, but I wasn't the least bit sleepy. I sat down under the lemon tree in the garden. I had a feeling of immense peace that contrasted sharply with the agitation I experienced in the United States. Over here, time had a slower rhythm, and life had another purpose: living.

"Thank you, Grandfather," I whispered. "Thank you for all the love you send me from Heaven."

# 23

The delightful carnival reminded me of one of the few holidays my family celebrated. My parents really didn't devote much time to holidays because they were always working. But on Thanksgiving, my parents couldn't work, even if they wanted to, because everything was closed. It's one of the most important traditional holidays in the U.S., a time for giving thanks to God for all the good gifts we've received, a time when family and friends gather to share the fruits of their labors, and to eat and drink.

On that day, my parents would invite our few friends over to our apartment. They would bring their relatives, and our apartment would fill up with children and adults. My mother would prepare a large turkey with a delicious special sauce. It took her all day to make the turkey, while my father and I cleaned house. At about five o'clock in the afternoon, the guests would begin to arrive, bringing more food, beer, and wine. My father would turn on loud music, and the party was underway.

During the party, I would stay in my room. From there I could hear the usual *cumbias*, the music my parents and their guests loved to dance to. I'd listen as the group burst out laughing at worn-out Pepito jokes, about a naughty, know-it-all little boy; these were jokes I had heard over and over at home, but I didn't find them funny.

The guests likely considered me a strange boy, but honestly, no matter how hard I tried to participate in the party, it was very difficult for me. The topics of conversation seemed foreign to me: the social and political situation in our homeland, the money they sent to relatives there, and many other things I didn't know or care much about. I felt far removed from all of that, although sometimes I made a sincere effort to participate in the conversation.

I truly lived in two worlds: one at home and another at school. The first was my parents' world, including everything related to their roots, their Spanish language, and their culture. The second was the U.S. culture I was growing up in: school, friends, English language, television, music, sports.

My parents' bodies were in the United States, but their hearts were in their homeland. Both my heart and my body were in the United States, but whenever I entered my house, my parents' world still affected me. It was as if I had stepped into a foreign land.

Sometimes they made me take part in the party, forcing me to come out of my room and dance *cumbias*. My mother would make me dance with her. She danced very well, but I just couldn't get the steps right, no matter how hard I tried. A little jump to the left and a hop to the right. Impossible. There was something about that music that just didn't inspire me to dance, and my movements were clumsy.

While the music played in the apartment and everyone danced, I'd slip away to my bedroom, lock the door, turn on the TV, and watch the Oakland Raiders.

Of course, I wouldn't miss dinner for anything. I wasn't *that* clumsy! When dinner was served, I was one of the first to the table. After my father said a long prayer mentioning all the members of the family, living and dead, he carved and served generous portions of turkey with Mom's delicious sauce. I'd find a way to squeeze rice, beans (had to have beans), and potato salad onto the plate too. Oh, and tortillas! All of this with a big glass of *horchata*. And afterward, the dessert: a large serving of delicious bundt cake. That was my favorite part of the party. The tasty meal erased my identity problems. At the table, we were all equal.

After dinner, more *cumbias* for everyone else and more football for me.

"*Cumbia, sabrosa cumbia . . .*"

"Touchdown!"

That's how my family celebrated Thanksgiving.

# 24

My aunt's voice awakened me; she was calling me for breakfast. I asked if we could eat in the garden, and she gladly agreed.

"I love the garden too," she said. "It's so cozy."

"I slept here last night."

"In the garden?"

"Yes."

"Weren't you afraid?" she asked.

"No. I had never slept outside in a hammock."

"It's so pleasant and comfortable."

"As if the angels were rocking me to sleep," I said.

The breakfast was delicious.

"Speaking of angels," she said, "didn't Flor de Ángel look beautiful last night?"

"Did she ever!" I replied, unable to hold back a smile.

"Do you like her?"

"She's a pretty girl."

"She's also very intelligent. And she has a strong personality."

"I think I'm in love," I blurted out.

"I can see that," my aunt said, smiling.

"How?" I asked. "What does a person in love look like?"

"When you're with Flor de Ángel, you only have eyes for her."

"That's true. Being by her side makes me happy. Is that good or bad?"

"It's natural."

"Forgive me, Aunt, but I trust you and want to ask you what I should do. What do you advise?"

"About what?"

"About my love for Flor de Ángel."

"If she feels the same, there's nothing more to talk about. It takes two," she said.

I felt I could talk about almost anything with my aunt, but I couldn't quite bring myself to repeat the words that Flor de Ángel had said to me that morning: "If you go, I'm going with you." They still rang in my ears like a declaration of love.

We finished eating and my aunt asked the inevitable question: "And when are you going back to the United States?"

I didn't answer right away, and she sensed my indecision. In a kind voice, she said, "Don't think I'm kicking you out! You can stay as long as you want. It's a great pleasure for me to have you here. This is your home."

"Thank you very much, Aunt. I feel happy here," I said, sighing. "I love this land and its people. It's a wonderland, just like Grandfather said. Life itself is lived and felt so differently here."

"We aren't rich in money, but we certainly aren't poor in spirit. That's why I can't understand how so many people can forget about this place, go so far away and never come back. Of course, we don't have the comforts and luxuries of the wealthy countries, but we live life to the fullest, because life is all we have."

"There's a lot of poverty, too," I said. "Last night, at the carnival, I saw a lot of beggars, many women and children asking for charity in order to eat, while others were enjoying life. It doesn't seem fair to me."

"You're right," said someone behind us. It was Flor de Ángel, whose face radiated light.

I stood up. "Good morning."

"Good morning," she said and kissed my aunt, who invited her to sit down.

"Would you like something to eat? A cup of coffee?"

"No, thank you. I was just coming to see if your grandson wanted to take a walk around town."

"Good idea," agreed my aunt. "There are some very nice places to see."

"I'd love to," I said. "I'd like to see more of the town."

"Let's go then," said Flor de Ángel.

We said goodbye to my aunt and headed for the town plaza.

# 25

It was a beautiful day, with a clear blue sky, cool breeze, and warm sunshine. Flor de Ángel glowed with energy and charm. Each of her movements had grace and a beautiful cadence.

"You're really pretty," I said to her.

She smiled happily. "Thank you. You're very handsome."

"Thanks. I didn't know that."

"Hadn't anyone ever told you that?"

"No one."

"Not even your girlfriend in the United States?" she asked.

"I don't have a girlfriend."

"Why not?"

"Because I never even thought about that before."

"With so many pretty girls over there, with faces like Hollywood actresses?"

"None of them is as pretty as you," I said, looking into her eyes.

"Liar."

"It's true!"

We walked toward the plaza, which was already bustling with the day's business activities in shops, stores and stands around the central square.

We stepped into some shops and later had lunch at an open-air market. In the afternoon, we went to the old church and its beautiful gardens. We sat down on a bench in the shade of the trees. The place was peaceful and pleasant.

A short time later, a woman and child dressed in rags came over and asked us for some money. I put a few coins into the woman's hand. She thanked me and went on her way.

"I've noticed there are a lot of beggars around here."

"There's a lot of poverty and very few jobs," she said. "All the wealth is in the hands of a few."

"Now I understand very well why my parents left."

"Your grandfather left for the same reason."

"And your parents, how are they?" I asked.

Her beautiful face seemed to cloud a bit.

"Forgive me," I said. "I didn't mean to ask an inappropriate question."

"That's okay," she said. "It's just that I'm not often asked that."

"Let's talk about something else."

"No, it's okay. I'm going to answer your question. How are my parents? Well . . . my father died in the civil war, and my mother was left with three children. In order to support us, she had to go to the capital, to do whatever kind of work she could find. My sister, brother, and I stayed with my grandma, or rather on our own, because she spends the whole day at church. In spite of all my mother's sacrifices to give us a decent life, my brother quit school and works when he can, which isn't often. He's become a total bum. My older sister is only eighteen and already has two children with different fathers."

"And what are you hoping to do in life?"

"I don't know. I just know that I don't want to be a bum like my brother or have fatherless children like my sister. I'm sure of that. I could get a job in the foreign assembly plants, but that's just allowing yourself to be exploited. One of my cousins works there. She says they only give you three minutes a day to go to the bathroom, and when you're gone longer than that, they take the time out of your check. Although she works hard six days a week, she has no rights or benefits, and they can fire her for any reason."

"Now I understand why you said, 'if you go, I'm going with you.' And I believed it was a declaration of love," I confessed, blushing.

"It is," she said, smiling. "It's a declaration of love and hope. I learned from my father to have faith. He died because he had faith that the world was going to change. I have faith that things will change. You're my love and my hope for the future."

Flor de Ángel sounded so sure of herself, so mature, despite her youth. This quality made her, in addition to beautiful, very special. The more I got to know her, the more she impressed me.

"I was planning to stay here," I said.

She didn't say a word.

I took her soft hand in mine and said, "But it looks like I should go back to the United States, and you want to go between me."

"That's right," she said, squeezing both of my hands between hers.

"It's easy for me to go back, because I have a plane ticket, a passport, and legal residency in the United States."

"And I don't have any of that. But I can find out how to get a passport, and we'll find a way to arrange the rest—you'll see!"

She said this with such determination that I was convinced it would happen. We continued our walk through town. Evening came, and the sunset was magnificent. The clouds were streaked with colors, and the entire town had an orange glow as the sun slowly slipped behind the mountain as if it were pulling down the curtain of day to give way to night.

After the sunset, I walked Flor de Ángel home, and we said goodnight with a soft kiss.

"Thanks for the walk," I said.

"Thanks for the hope," she replied.

"Goodnight."

"See you tomorrow."

"Goodbye."

# 26

My aunt was waiting for me with dinner on the table, along with a distinguished-looking visitor. She introduced him.

"Sergio, this is Moisés, an old friend of your grandfather."

I went over to shake his hand.

"Maybe you don't remember me," he said, "but I met you when you were little. Your grandfather and I had great adventures together. We traveled together to work on building the Panama Canal."

Moisés was pleasant, with a resolute attitude. He reminded me very much of Grandfather.

"Dinner's ready," said my aunt. "Come to eat!"

We sat down at the table and had a lively, pleasant conversation as we ate. Moisés had a lot of stories to tell, and my aunt and I listened attentively.

"Moisés used to take people to the United States," she commented

"Yes," he said. "It wasn't an easy job, but it was a lot of fun."

"Fun?" my aunt asked in amazement. "I'd say dangerous! I would never dare make that trip."

"You have to know what you're doing," said Moisés. "There are safe routes. I'm proud to say I never exploited anyone, and none of my travelers was ever lost or died on the way. They all reached their destinations safely and without getting caught by Immigration."

"It's obvious you have a lot of experience," I said, "and that you treated people well. My parents had bad luck."

"I know your parents' story," said Moisés. "I was supposed to take them, but I got sick and they went with another guide who didn't know what he was doing."

"Why don't you make those trips anymore?" I asked him.

"Because I'm too old for that. Your grandfather was in one of my last groups. Now I raise pigs. It's a peaceful occupation. The pigs don't complicate my life, and they feed me."

We finished eating and Moisés got up.

"Thank you for dinner," he said. "It was delicious. Now I should go home to bed, because pigs are early risers, and I have to take care of them."

Moisés turned to me and said, "It's so nice to see you all grown up, a real young man! Rest assured that I'm at your service for anything you might need."

"Thank you very much. It's very nice to have met you. You remind me a lot of Grandfather."

"We got along very well. He was a good man."

Moisés hugged my aunt, shook my hand, and left.

"Good night."

"Good night."

I helped my aunt clear the table and wash the dishes. Then we went back out to the garden to continue our conversation.

"Did you and Flor de Ángel have a nice walk?"

"Yes, we walked and talked a lot. She told me the story

of her life," I said, remembering the sad fate of Flor de
Ángel's family.

"She's a very bright girl, but she has no future here. It
would be a real shame for her intelligence to be wasted.
There are no opportunities here unless you know influen-
tial people. We poor people can only hope to barely getting by. Flor de Ángel deserves better than that."

"She wants to go to the United States," I commented.

"I know, I myself have advised her to try to find a way
to do it."

"She wants to go with me."

"It's not a bad idea."

"For me it's easy to go back because I have my airline
ticket, passport, and legal residency in the United States.
But she doesn't have any of that."

My aunt thought for a moment and then had an idea:
"You go by plane, and she can travel by land with one of
the many groups that leave here every day. Then you can
meet up again in the United States. I think that's the best
solution, don't you?"

"The trip by land is dangerous."

"Flor de Ángel is intelligent."

"But she needs protection."

"The guide and the other travelers will protect her,"
my aunt assured me. "And you can help her get estab-
lished over there. Do you know who can give you advice
about this?"

"Who?"

"Moisés."

"Good idea, Tía. I'll talk to him tomorrow."

We went on talking about a lot of other things in that
pleasant garden until it got late and we went to bed.

My concern for Flor de Ángel's future did not let me sleep. Suddenly an idea occurred to me that at first seemed ridiculous, but the more I thought about it, the more reasonable it seemed. And that allowed me to finally fall asleep.

# 27

The next morning I got up early and, after having breakfast with my aunt, I went to Flor de Ángel's house. She wasn't home, and her grandmother wasn't sure when she would be back. I asked her to tell Flor de Ángel that I'd come back in a couple of hours. Meanwhile, I took advantage of the time to go visit Moisés. I found him busy feeding the pigs, and who should be helping him but Flor de Ángel! We were surprised to see each other and greeted each other with a kiss.

"I see you two already know each other!" said the old man, smiling.

"Yes, we've known each other a few days now," she replied.

I watched a group of pigs, and said, "They look very healthy."

"Pigs are calm and, as long as they have enough to eat, that's all they care about."

Moisés was tossing food to the animals. He stopped for a moment, and asked me, "What can I do for you, young man? I imagine you aren't here just to talk about pigs with this old man. You must have something else on your mind."

"I wanted to ask you about something, but I don't know if Flor de Ángel already did."

"Yes," she said. "That's exactly what we were talking about."

"I already gave her my advice," said Moisés, "about getting a passport, a guide, and money. I think she can get everything together in a week."

"I'm worried about Flor de Ángel's safety," I said. "I know the trip by land can be very dangerous."

"If you go with an experienced guide, it's quite safe; there are fewer risks," said Moisés.

Then I brought up the idea that had occurred to me the night before, "I'll go with her."

She looked at me in surprise: "But your papers are in order to go back by plane," she said, "and you have legal residence in the United States. There's no need for you to expose yourself to danger."

"Flor de Ángel is right," Moisés said. "You shouldn't take unnecessary risks."

"It's my decision," I said. "This way Flor de Ángel won't go alone."

She smiled happily and threw herself into my arms. "With you by my side, I'll feel safer. I appreciate you going with me."

"Fine," said Moisés. "I understand that the next group will leave in a week. Go sign up right away, so you'll have enough time to get ready."

We said goodbye to Moisés. Flor de Ángel looked very happy.

"This will be the trip of my dreams," she said excitedly as we walked through town.

We followed Moisés's instructions and signed up for the next trip. We were told to pay at least half the total cost of the trip on the day of departure, or the whole amount, depending on the arrangement under which we were traveling.

Then we went to give the news to my aunt and Flor de Ángel's grandmother. They both seemed pleased that I was going to accompany her.

We spent the whole week getting ready for the trip and coming up with the money to pay for Flor de Ángel's trip. Borrowing from several people, we managed to get the necessary amount.

We visited the local landmarks for the last time, which caused our feelings for each other to deepen. The trip had become the constant topic of conversation. It was a big adventure for us.

I wrote a long letter to my parents explaining the plans for my return trip. I knew they would not approve and would probably think I had lost my mind. I explained that I was going to travel by land in order to accompany Flor de Ángel, that she was my girlfriend, and that I hoped they would understand my concern for her safety. I was sure that all of this was going to surprise and annoy them.

I had accomplished the mission of laying Grandfather to rest in his land. Now I felt that it was my duty to go with Flor de Ángel and help her enter the United States so that her dreams of a better life could come true. I could already imagine the frustration the letter would cause my father. I just hoped that my mother would understand and intercede on my behalf as she had always done.

I also sent a letter to the counselor to let her know about Grandfather's burial and to tell her about Flor de Ángel and my new plans of returning by land with her.

# 28

That day, I received a letter from the counselor. She wrote with great optimism because construction of the new Belmont High had finally been approved. Mrs. Berenson also included a couple of clippings from Los Angeles newspapers explaining the details.

I was very pleased to get this news and just hoped that further problems would not come up this time, since construction had already been postponed twice. First, toxic gases were discovered on the land, and then a seismic fault was discovered on a site that already had buildings. Because it was impossible to determine whether the fault was active, the authorities decided to cancel the project for the second time.

According to the news stories, the Vista Hermosa project, as the plan was called, was approved by a majority of the members of the Los Angeles Unified School District board.

Up until that time, the construction had already taken six years at a cost of $175 million. It was estimated that the new phase would be completed in four years and would cost $111 million more. If completed, it would be a total of ten years at an approximate price of $286 million, which would make Belmont the most expensive public school in the United States.

The new high school would serve 2,600 students, and

its facilities would include a park, an auditorium, a cafeteria, a library, and two activity centers, one for parents and another for students. The library and park would be open to the public. The park would have a lake, a soccer field, an open-air theater, and walking paths.

I imagined that the students, teachers, and parents would be very happy, since we would finally have a new school which, among many positive things, would lift the spirits of the young people and the community.

The newspapers reported very favorable reactions: "We've been waiting more than twenty years for a good school. How great that we will finally have it," said one of the many neighborhood residents. This resident had helped to convince the members of the school board that the need for the school was greater than the environmental problems involving the land on which it would be built. "This makes our dreams of a good education, social justice, equality, and opportunity for all a reality," said another resident.

Right then and there I sent Mrs. Berenson a postcard to greet her and thank her for the news. I congratulated her for her efforts. She was one of the people who had taken a personal interest in encouraging students and parents to get involved in the project and participate in discussions on whether construction of the new school should continue. That woman was a true example of selflessness. She was always present at the meetings with political leaders in order to make sure that the interests of the students were not forgotten.

# 29

When I woke up the next day, I was alone at my aunt's house. She was out running errands. I was making good use of the time, packing for the trip. The guide had told us that we should pack one pair of pants, one shirt, and our personal hygiene items in a small bag. That was all. We were not to take anything more than necessary.

Suddenly, the house began to shake violently and move from side to side like a ship on rough seas. I heard a strange noise and a buzzing sound that rattled my nerves.

At that moment, all I wanted to do was run out of the house, but I couldn't because my legs were frozen with fear and my feet felt glued to the floor, which kept moving.

Things began to fall to the floor: books, shelves, dishes, pots and pans. My terror increased when I heard the neighbors shouting "Earthquake!"

I thought the house was going to collapse and trap me inside, since my body was still paralyzed with panic. At that instant I felt someone take me by the hand and pull me toward the door. Without a doubt, I knew that at that critical moment that Grandfather had come to rescue me.

When I finally managed to get outside, I saw many other terrified people. Then I realized that it was dangerous out there too, because the earthquake had grown stronger and the power poles and electrical cables were swinging back and forth and falling.

It was all happening so fast, yet the fear made each second feel like an eternity. Everything was shaking, and it felt like the whole world was crashing down. I thought of running away, but instead decided to go back to the house. The movement stopped then, and the earth stood still, but the atmosphere of panic remained. I joined a group of neighbors, all crying in despair, and I cried with them. Someone was screaming that the world was coming to an end. A little boy was crying, looking for his mother. A woman was shouting that she didn't want to die.

Until that moment, concerned with my own safety, I had not thought about my aunt and Flor de Ángel, and I asked God to keep them safe.

Then Flor de Ángel emerged from the crowd of people milling about in the street, and I calmed down somewhat. Her beautiful face was full of worry. I rushed over to her and put my arms around her.

"Are you all right?" I asked.

"Yes, thank God," she said.

"And your family?"

"They're all okay. Some houses in my neighborhood collapsed, but fortunately ours is still standing."

"The earthquake was terrible here. I was in the house when it started, and I thought the walls were going to collapse on me."

"And your aunt?"

"I don't know where she is! She went out to run some errands and isn't back yet."

"Here I am!" we heard my aunt shout.

Flor de Ángel and I rushed over and embraced her.

"It's unbelievable," she said, frightened. "Entire neighborhoods have been destroyed."

Suddenly the earth shook again, and we were again overcome with terror. When the shaking stopped, the three of us hugged and comforted each other.

"There are a lot of people who need help," Flor de Ángel said. "I'm going to go see how I can help."

"Good idea," I said. "I'll go with you."

But at that moment I thought about my aunt. "Wait a minute, let me walk my aunt back to her house first."

"I hope it didn't collapse," she said.

Fearlessly, Flor de Ángel walked right into the house, and we followed her.

"A lot of things fell down," she said. "But the house looks fine."

"Praise the Lord," said my aunt thankfully. "You can tell this house is well built. When I was coming back from downtown, I saw so many homes that had collapsed."

We picked the things up off the floor and straightened up. Once everything was in place, my aunt wanted to watch the news.

"The TV won't turn on," she said. "The radio either."

"There's no power because of the earthquake," Flor de Ángel confirmed.

It was noon by the time Flor de Ángel and I went out into the neighborhood to offer our help to those less fortunate. Some parts of town were true scenes of destruction. Many houses had collapsed, and people were trying to rescue some of their possessions from the ruins. Those of us who were able worked on rescuing people from the rubble and helping the wounded.

Before dark we went to check on Flor de Ángel's family, and then we went back to my aunt's house. The power was back on, and she was watching in horror as the news showed scenes of the devastation caused by the earthquake. At first a lot of people thought it was just a simple temblor, the kind that are common in this country called "Valley of the Hammocks." No one imagined that it was a disaster of great proportions. In the blink of an eye, that land of color and enchantment had been invaded by tragedy.

The news was reporting that in most of the country there was no water, electricity, or telephone service. There was no gasoline. Businesses were closed. Everyone was overcome by a desperate sensation of isolation, unable to learn the fate of relatives in other parts of the country. People had to resign themselves to praying and waiting.

From that moment on, nothing was the same. An intense generalized fear pervaded the atmosphere, deepening every time the earth shook again. At the slightest tremor, people screamed and ran. Temblors of varying degrees of intensity were felt during the rest of the day and through the night until dawn. It was impossible to rest or relax. The safest places to sleep were outside, on the sidewalk, or in the park.

I tried to call my parents, but all the phone lines were busy. I could imagine how worried they must have been, I kept trying to reach them, but it was impossible. I knew they would be anxiously awaiting my call, like thousands of others who were trying day and night to reach their relatives. There was no choice but to wait for the phone lines to be available. During those sad moments, the company of my aunt and Flor de Ángel was my only consolation.

# 30

The next day I was finally able to get through to my parents on the phone. My mother answered immediately and screamed when she heard my voice.

"My son! How are you? Where are you? Are you okay? Why haven't you called us?"

"Forgive me, Mamá. I didn't want you to worry, but the lines have been busy since yesterday. It's been impossible to get through."

"But how are you?" my father asked from the other phone. "Are you okay?"

"Thank God, I'm all right," I said right away. "Nothing happened to me or my aunt. Her house didn't collapse. But many areas of the country suffered serious damage and many people died."

"Yes," Mom said, "there are complete newsreports about the earthquake here. It's so sad! Our poor country! It seems like even God has forgotten those unfortunate people."

"The earth is still shaking," I said. "In fact, it's shaking right now."

I immediately regretted having told my mother that, because she screamed in fear, "Oh my God! How awful!"

"Go to a safe place!" shouted my father.

"It stopped," I reassured them. "There have been a lot of aftershocks like this one, so people have been sleeping outside."

"Be careful that nothing bad happens to you," said Mamá. "I'm going to light a candle to San Martín de Porres to protect you."

"There are a lot of people who need emergency aid," I said.

"Groups are organizing here in Los Angeles to collect donations and send them immediately," my father assured me.

"I hope they're able to gather a lot, because it's really needed."

In the end I was able to convince my parents that I was safe. They felt a little better, and we said goodbye. To be honest, though, things were very unstable, and the entire country was still in a state of emergency. I took advantage of the phone call to tell them that I had mailed them a letter explaining in detail the change of plans for my return to the United States, and to watch the mail so the letter wouldn't get lost.

The television stations continued broadcasting scenes of devastation and tragedy. My aunt, Flor de Ángel, and I watched openmouthed, unable to believe the terrible images. The reports detailed the high number of traumatized people searching for their loved ones. Men and women wandered through the shelters, looking for their parents and children. Others, obviously shaken, walked back and forth carrying the few possessions they had been able to rescue from the rubble.

Meanwhile, our trip to the United States had been postponed because several places along the highway were closed by landslides. They estimated that we would leave about two weeks late, or as soon as the roads were open.

Despite the disaster, the local residents were striving to return to a normal life. They buried their dead and repaired their homes, when possible. They seemed to be accustomed to calamities and did not allow the earthquake to destroy their love of life. That was what impressed me most about those people, Grandfather's people, my people.

# 31

When the roads were finally reopened, we were informed that our group would be leaving for the United States soon. Our departure day came, and I said goodbye to my aunt with tears in my eyes.

"Thank you for all the happiness you've given me," she said. "I'll never forget you and I hope you'll come back soon. You have a home here, and an aunt who loves you very much."

"Thank you, Tía," I said with emotion. "I never dreamed that here I would meet a person as dear and full of life as you." I kissed her forehead. "Goodbye, Tía."

"Goodbye, son. God bless you."

I went to Flor de Ángel's house. Together we visited Grandfather's grave and placed a wreath of flowers on it. I asked Grandfather for his blessing and protection for our journey. A great sense of calm filled me, knowing he was resting in the bosom of his beloved homeland, his dying wish. Now it was time for me to return to my adopted country and take Flor de Ángel with me.

The first surprise of our trip was meeting Moisés at our departure point.

"Thank you for coming to see us off," I told him.

"No," he said, "I'm not here to see you off, but to accompany you. I'm going to be your guide."

"I'm so glad!" exclaimed Flor de Ángel. "But I thought you didn't make these trips anymore."

"This will be my last one. I want to make sure you get there safely. I dreamed about your grandfather last night, and in the dream he was asking me a big favor. It wasn't too clear what it was, but when I woke up, I realized he was asking me to protect you two on this journey. The only way I can do that is to take you myself. So I'll be the guide for this group. We'll be leaving soon."

The twenty-seven members of the group all rejoiced at this news, since we all knew of the old man's reputation as one of the best guides for undocumented people going to the United States.

Moisés looked each of us over to be sure we were all wearing dark clothing and comfortable walking shoes, as we had been instructed when we signed up for the trip.

All we could bring with us was one backpack or small suitcase with one change of clothes. Flor de Ángel and I had paid for the trip in advance, at a special price because we were friends of Moisés. In some cases, people paid half prior to departure and the other half would be paid by the traveler's relatives in the United States before the group crossed the border or before the traveler was turned over to his or her relatives.

Moisés told us to get on the bus. Everyone was excited. Flor de Ángel and I sat in front. The vehicle pulled away. When we had left the town, Moisés stood up and spoke to the group.

"First of all, I want to tell you not to worry, to leave everything to me and follow my instructions exactly. That way everything will go fine. I know you want to make it to the United States, and that's what you've paid me for. Rest assured that you will arrive there without any problems. But I do insist that you do what I say to avoid being lost or having an accident."

He paused and then shouted: "Understood?"

We all answered: "Understood!"

"Good. I see that you're paying attention. You're good passengers. Now I'll explain the route we're going to follow. With me there are no secrets. I want you all to know the details of the trip. And if you have any questions, please don't hesitate to ask."

Someone commented, "I don't speak English."

"You don't have to," said Moisés. "Our contacts in the United States speak English perfectly. They'll take care of everything."

"Thank you," said the passenger.

"One part of the route we'll be taking will be by land," Moisés continued. "And another is by sea. And finally we'll cross a river."

"I can't swim!" cried a woman.

"Don't worry," said Moisés. "We'll travel by boat for the sea portion of the trip, and the river isn't deep. We have everything figured out so that you won't be in any danger."

"What is the exact route?" a man wanted to know.

"I'll explain it to you on the way," Moisés answered. "Pay attention. Our first objective is to reach Cahuites, a fishing town in Oaxaca, early tomorrow morning."

"Where?" someone asked.

"Oaxaca. It's spelled O-a-x-a-c-a and pronounced *Wah-hah-kah*. It's in Mexico. During the first part of the trip, we'll cross Guatemala and the Mexican border. So we have a twenty-four-hour bus ride ahead of us. Rest, sleep, and don't worry."

# 32

After a long ride, the bus stopped at the Guatemalan border. Moisés told us what papers to fill out and what information to include to get through Customs and Immigration. We took advantage of the stop to use the bathroom and get something to eat. After an hour, we got back on the bus and proceeded into Guatemalan territory.

"We've crossed the first border," said Moisés. "That's the easiest one. Next comes the Mexican border, which is not the easiest nor the most difficult."

Moisés returned to his seat, across from the one where Flor de Ángel and I were sitting.

"This is the same route your grandfather traveled to the United States," he said. "I remember he was so happy and looking forward to getting there. He said that although he had already lived a long time and had many experiences, he felt the United States was going to give him new energy to live his final years. That's what your grandfather said. He invited me to visit him over there, but I was always busy and I never did. During the civil war, people left in droves. There weren't enough guides. People were desperate and went with anybody, even inexperienced guides. The guides would cheat people and leave them stranded. I took groups of thirty people every ten days. There was a lot of business."

"And nowadays," asked Flor de Ángel, "do many people go North?"

"There are always people who go to seek their fortune in other countries," Moisés answered. "In the past they left for fear of dying in the war. Now it's for fear of starving to death."

"Grandfather never wanted to go back," I said.

"That's what he had in mind. He planned to make a new life for himself in the North. And I believe he achieved that, because he didn't come back except to be buried."

"That's right," I said.

Moisés leaned back in his seat. "I'm going to close my eyes for awhile," he said. "We have a long trip ahead of us and we have to rest every chance we get."

"Okay, have a good rest," I said.

"Thank you."

Flor de Ángel was looking out the window at the green landscape, her gaze lost in the distance. I took her hand in mine. She looked at me with her big, dark eyes. Her face beamed with a mysterious smile.

"What are you thinking about?" I whispered into her ear, as my lips brushed against her beautiful, fragrant hair.

"You," she said somewhat flirtatiously.

That unexpected response surprised me a little, and I asked, "Why?"

"Because you had the option of going back on a quick, comfortable flight, and I don't know why you chose to come on this slow, noisy bus."

"Ah, but I'm with you, and nothing compares to that!"

"Are you sure?"

"Of course. Besides, I wouldn't want anything to happen to you, and I can protect you."

"Nothing bad will happen to us. Remember, we're traveling with Moisés," she reminded me.

"Yes, then we'll have a good trip in every way."

"God willing."

We continued chatting about many aspects of our lives. I realized that Flor de Ángel was not only my girlfriend but also my friend. I could talk to her about anything in complete confidence. I talked to her about life in the United Sates, my parents, my friends, my school, the differences between the two countries, the people there, the language. She seemed very interested in all of it and asked me a lot of questions.

Night had fallen, and the dark road was brightened only by the bus's headlights. The passengers rode along in silence, many of them sleeping.

Hours later, the driver announced that we were approaching the Mexican border. Moisés awakened everyone and told us what papers to fill out and what to say when asked about our reasons for traveling to Mexico.

"You have to say that we're on a tour. I'll give each of you a tourist information sheet that shows the places we will supposedly visit, such as Oaxaca, Acapulco, Puebla, Mexico City, Xochimilco, and Guadalajara. You also have to say that you work for International Textiles Inc. and that this tour is part of a special program the company has for its employees. All this is included on the tourist information sheet, the places we'll visit and the hotels in which we're supposedly going to be staying. If any of you have any problems, I'll be nearby if you need me. I'll explain everything. Understood?"

"Yes," we all answered.

"Usually there's no problem with tourist trips, but sometimes the passengers get scared when they talk and contradict themselves. Don't be afraid. Talk. And if you need help, I'll be there. Remember, I'm your tourist guide. And I'll take care of everything with Immigration and Customs. Okay, we're here. Now get off the bus and follow me as if we were on a tour. And don't get lost."

Everything went just as Moisés had said. We got through Customs, used the restrooms, purchased food, and continued on our way. When we had traveled a distance from the border, Moisés addressed us again. "See how easy that was? That's because you all followed my instructions exactly. Excellent. Now we're in Mexico, heading for Cahuites, the fishing town I told you about this morning. We'll arrive early in the morning. So get some sleep. When we get to Cahuites, I'll tell you what we're going to do next. Good night."

# 33

We arrived in Cahuites, and the bus stopped on a deserted street. The town was dark and silent. The driver turned off the vehicle's headlights. Moisés awakened the passengers.

"I hope you've gotten enough sleep. Now I'll explain the next step. You'll remember that I told you that part of the trip would be by sea. Well, the time has come."

"Why do we have to go by sea?" a woman asked.

"Will we go by boat?" a man asked.

"Good questions," Moisés said as he stood in the dark interior of the bus. "The reason for traveling a short piece of the journey by sea is to bypass two police checkpoints that always cause a lot of trouble for people going north. They demand a lot of money to let you go through, and that would make the trip too expensive. Sometimes they arrest people and refuse to let them go unless they pay a huge sum of money. So, to avoid that, we'll get off here, take a boat to the port of Salinas Cruz, and a bus will be waiting there to take us to the U.S. border. Understood?"

"Yes!" we answered.

"Very well. So get off slowly, in order, and without making any noise. I'll take you to the place where we'll get on the boat."

Moisés got off the bus and waited. When we had all gotten off, we followed him down the moonlit path toward the shore.

A man was waiting on a small dock. He handed Moisés the key for the craft, which was floating nearby. Moisés gave the man some money, and the man took it and left without saying a word.

One by one we climbed aboard.

"It's small," one man said.

"Don't worry," Moisés urged us. "It's a shark-hunting boat, strong enough to hold thirty people. Get in and make yourselves comfortable as best you can. No one can remain standing."

Moisés gestured to me and Flor de Ángel to wait: "You two will sit by me," he said quietly.

When all the passengers were seated, Moisés climbed aboard, followed by Flor de Ángel and me. It must have been about three o'clock in the morning when the craft pulled away from the dock.

"We won't go far from shore, just a mile or so, to avoid being detected," Moisés informed us.

"How long is the trip?" a man asked.

"We'll be at the port in two hours. We'll go slowly."

"It looks like rain," someone commented.

"It already rained," Moisés confirmed. "That's why the air still smells like rain."

Flor de Ángel was trembling from the cold. I moved closer to her and put my arm around her to keep her warm.

"The sea is a little rough from the rain," said Moisés. "Hang on tight so you don't fall in. And don't reach outside the boat or touch the water. We don't want to attract sharks."

We were quite far from shore now and could see the land only faintly in the distance.

"We'll be in Salinas Cruz by dawn," said Moisés. "That's the plan."

At that moment, Flor de Ángel screamed in terror and pointed. When I turned to look, all I saw was an enormous wave coming down on us like a huge mountain of water.

"Hang on tight!" Moisés shouted.

With one hand he grabbed me, and I clung to Flor de Ángel. The next thing I knew we were caught up in a strong current of water that pulled us out of the boat and down into a violent whirlpool, our bodies spinning crazily and colliding with one another.

Struggling back to the surface, the water now calm, I swam to where Flor de Ángel and Moisés were floating, not far from the boat. We joined him and other passengers and, assisting each other, climbed back on board. Moisés tried to start the motor, which was flooded, but after several tries, he managed to get it going. Then he checked to make sure everyone was on board. It was obvious that several people were missing.

"My husband's gone!" A woman screamed desperately.

"Don't worry; we'll find him," said Moisés. "We'll circle the area to rescue him."

"Over there, there's some people swimming!" someone noticed.

Indeed, two men were swimming toward the boat, and with our help they climbed back aboard.

"We thought we had lost you," a man said. Then he pointed across the water and added, "There are some bodies floating there. Maybe they didn't know how to swim and swallowed too much water."

Moisés steered the boat in that direction, but we didn't find anyone. The water was so dark that we couldn't see anything. He counted the passengers and concluded that three were missing, including the husband of one of the survivors. The woman begged him to continue searching for her husband, and we did so, but to no avail.

"We've searched a long time and there's no one here," said Moisés. "We have to continue on. I'm sorry for those who've been lost; this was a terrible accident."

The woman tried to throw herself into the water, but other passengers held her back.

"Calm down, friend," one of them said to her. "Maybe he survived and the waves carried him back to shore."

Moisés added, "When we reach the port, I'll get in touch with my contacts in Cahuites and they'll let us know if they've found anyone."

"Please, God, let them find him," prayed the woman, "because without my husband, there's no reason to go on. Our dream was to make a new life together in the United States and provide for our children. But without him, it's not worth it."

We were crowded in the boat, now completely soaked and trembling with cold, frightened after the tremendous impact of the gigantic wave. Flor de Ángel and I kept our arms around each other to stay warm amid those waters whipped by a strong, cold wind, whose whistling sounded like a scream of despair.

No one spoke. At that tragic time, words lacked meaning, and we had not recovered from the brutal whipping of that mountain of water.

Moisés steered the boat in silence, his gaze focused on the treacherous sea.

The wife of one of the lost men began sobbing again, and another passenger consoled her, "Don't cry. You'll see, when we reach the port, we'll get news of your husband."

"God willing!" said the woman sighing. "God willing!"

I squeezed Flor de Ángel's hand, and thought about Grandfather. She caressed my head and I softly kissed her forehead. In my mind I heard Grandfather's voice telling me, "Don't worry, beloved grandson, everything's fine. The danger has passed."

The vessel continued its journey across the sea, now in calm.

"There's the port of Salinas Cruz," said Moisés, pointing toward a bright spot on the coast. "We're almost there."

"May God bless those who are missing," said a woman. "Let's hope they made it to shore alive."

# 34

We went ashore at the port at daybreak. Most of us had lost our backpacks and suitcases, and we felt very uncomfortable in our wet clothes and shoes.

We went to a restaurant, where we were served a big, tasty breakfast. We stayed there for a couple of hours, waiting for a clothing store to open. The owner of the store knew Moisés and gave us a discount on everything we bought.

Fortunately, we still had money. We had all followed Moisés's instructions, so our cash was wrapped in plastic, tied to our belts, and hidden inside our pants. The women had plastic bags of cash in their bras. These were the instructions for protecting our money and documents.

After having breakfast and putting on dry clothes, most of the passengers had regained their enthusiasm. Flor de Ángel's smile was back, which made me happy. I had been close to losing her at sea, and I didn't even want to think what I would have done if that had happened.

Moisés was not able to reach his contacts in Cahuites, and the woman who had lost her husband, in despair, decided to return by bus to that fishing town in search of her loved one. We all wished her the best of luck. Moisés returned the payment for the trip to her, hers as well as her husband's.

"There are four less people in our group now," said the old man. "But we must continue on. We should go back to the restaurant now. Follow me."

We had coffee and soft drinks at the restaurant. The place was empty, except for our group. I suspected that it was a special place for travelers headed to the United States.

Moisés stood up and addressed the group. "Well, as you can see, we've had a very difficult time. Thank God, we have survived. In an hour, we'll be picked up by the bus that will take us to the U.S. border. It's a four-day trip. We'll stop in Guadalajara, Guaymas, Hermosillo, and finally in Tijuana."

"And when are we going to cross the border to the United States?" a woman asked.

"That's the last step," Moisés replied. "We'll talk about that once we get to Tijuana. Then I'll explain all the details. For now, get ready for the four-day trip through Mexico. Use the restrooms, and eat as much as you like if you're still hungry. I'll tell you when the bus gets here."

Some people got up and went to use the restrooms. Others paced back and forth in the restaurant, smoking nervously and talking about the gigantic wave that had crashed down on us at sea.

Moisés sat down by Flor de Ángel and me, away from the other travelers. "Are you feeling all right?"

Flor de Ángel said yes, but that she still had not fully recovered from the scare at sea.

"What a strange thing!" Moisés commented. "Nothing like that has ever happened to me before. I've crossed that stretch of water more than fifty times. The time I brought your grandfather, we were circled by a huge blue shark, but the beast didn't hurt us and finally it swam away. . . . That damn wave was enormous. It's a miracle we didn't all drown, and that the boat didn't sink. I feel so bad about the three who were lost."

"I think someone is protecting us from above," I said.

"I'm sure it's Grandfather."

"Yes, someone who loves us very much," said Flor de Ángel. "Because otherwise we'd be at the bottom of the sea."

"Poor woman who lost her husband," I said. "She's a wreck."

"Who wouldn't be?" said Moisés. "She started out full of hopes and dreams, and in a matter of minutes they were swallowed up by the sea."

When the others returned, Moisés addressed the group again.

"The bus will be here soon, and I want to tell you that, although it's going to Tijuana, we won't be the only passengers. That is, there'll be other people on the bus who've come with other guides from other places. People from all over the world who are trying to enter the United States without papers disembark here at Salinas Cruz. It wouldn't be surprising if there were Chinese, Indian, and even European people on this bus, as well as people from all over Latin America, and especially Mexico. So we'll be sharing the bus with other travelers, but we all have the same destination. . . ."

Then he pointed. "I think that's the bus. So let's be ready to get on. Don't forget to follow my instructions. If we're stopped by the police on the way, let the guides take care of everything. Don't get off unless they, or we, tell you to. Get off the bus only at the places that I say you can, understand?

"Yes!" we all answered.

"Okay, then, let's get on the bus."

# 35

We got on the bus and, as Moisés had said, there were other passengers already aboard. All the seats in the front were taken, so we had to sit near the back. Flor de Ángel and I were the last ones to get on. We sat near a young mother and her little girl. Flor de Ángel immediately started making a fuss over the little one. The baby smiled happily, which made her mother feel comfortable with us.

I figured that the young mother was not more than eighteen years old. She reminded me of some of the girls at my school who became mothers at a very young age.

"How old is your little girl?" Flor de Ángel asked.

"She just turned a year and a half," said the mother.

"She's really pretty," I said.

"She's a real handful. She loves to play and isn't afraid of anyone. She's not shy at all."

"That's a sign of good health," said Flor de Ángel.

"It's because of her that I'm going to Tijuana . . . to see if I can cross the border to the United States, to try to give her a decent life. There's no hope in the town I'm from. There's nothing but hunger and poverty. It's a ghost town. Everyone has gone north and there are only old people and children left. I want my daughter to be somebody. But if we stay in my town, she'll end up ignorant like me and fall victim to unscrupulous man. That's why she and I are going north."

"And her father?" I asked.

"He left to work in Oregon when I was pregnant. He's never met his daughter. He sent us the money to go to Tijuana and cross the border with a man who will take us to Oregon."

"That's great!" said Flor de Ángel. "It's all set then."

"I hope so," replied the young mother. "They say that over there you work hard but live decently. And I'm willing to do anything for my daughter."

The bus, meanwhile, had already pulled away from Salinas Cruz. Moisés came over to us and said, "We won't go through Mexico City. We'll avoid the big-city police. Plus, we'll get to the border faster. We will not stop until we get to Guadalajara, which will take a whole day."

We were traveling along without any trouble. Moisés sat down near us to talk and later returned to his seat. Flor de Ángel and I talked up a storm, as Grandfather liked to say. The more we got to know each other, the more our love grew. The trip was an exciting adventure for me, and I was sure she felt the same way.

Flor de Ángel was helping the young mother, Jimena, with little Amanda. The two girls had grown very comfortable with each other during the long trek, as had Flor de Ángel with little Amanda. I even took a turn holding her while Jimena and Flor de Ángel slept.

This is how we spent the long journey through Mexico. We stopped at all the designated places, where we would eat, use the restrooms, and stretch our legs, as the driver got gas for the bus.

After four days we arrived in Tijuana, on the border with California.

Before we got off the bus, Moisés stood up and said, "I want to tell you that my part of the trip ends here. From here on you'll be with other guides, with whom you'll cross the border. They'll tell you everything you need to do. Follow their instructions and you'll soon be in the North, as promised. You'll be staying in a hotel here, four people per room, until your relatives in the United States pay the other half of the cost of the trip. Those who pay will then be taken across the border. So when you call your relatives, tell them to pay soon so that you can get to the other side quickly. Those of you who have already paid for the whole trip will cross the border tomorrow."

Once we were settled in the room we shared with Jimena and Amanda, Moisés came by and talked to us for a long time. He gave us all the details on the rest of the trip and told us we could trust our next guide, who was an old friend of his. Before he left, he gave us each a warm hug. Then, smiling, he said the pigs were waiting for him at home, and he left.

# 36

"When will you cross the border?" Jimena asked us while holding Amanda in her arms.

"Tomorrow," I replied. "How about you?"

"As soon as my husband pays."

"That's good."

Carrying Amanda, Jimena left the room to go to the hotel office, where the arrangements of the border crossings were handled. A short while later, she returned to the room crying.

"What happened?" asked Flor de Ángel. "Is something wrong with Amanda?"

"They don't want to take us across!" Jimena answered, disconsolate.

"Why not? Didn't your husband pay?" I asked her.

"None of the guides wants to be responsible for me because of Amanda. They say that taking a baby across is too risky. So no one will take us."

Jimena was crying, and little Amanda was too, seeing her mother's tears.

"I don't want to go back to my hometown. I have to cross the border any way I can to join my husband. He's waiting for us in Oregon."

I went to the office and talked to the guide for our group.

"I can't help her," he said. "She's going to Oregon, and I'm not familiar with that route. I only take people to Los

Angeles, Houston, and Washington, D.C."

"Why don't you help her? Can't you bring her along with us tomorrow?" I begged.

"Because it's not just a matter of getting her across the border. After that, someone has to take her to Oregon. That's the problem, because other guides cover that route. It's not my territory. The best thing for her to do is find a guide who's willing to help her cross the border and take her to Oregon."

I returned to our room and explained the situation to Jimena. She became even more discouraged. She just didn't know anyone in Tijuana that might be able to help her.

Our guide announced that everything would be ready for us to cross the border the following day. We told him that we had decided not to go with him and instead try to find someone who would take Jimena and Amanda.

"You don't know what a mess you're getting yourselves into," our guide said. "No *coyote* with any brains is going to agree to take a woman with a little baby across the border."

"We'll find one," Flor de Ángel said. "They say you can find anything here in Tijuana."

The next morning the guide organized the group. Before he left, he handed me a piece of paper with a name and phone number on it.

"I think this man might be able to help you," he said. "But I want you to understand that I don't know him and I don't know if he does a good job. All I know is that he deals with high-risk cases, like crossing with old people, children, and criminals. I'm giving you this information only because you are friends of Moisés, and he's my friend. Good luck, and be very careful. Remember, don't trust anyone. Be prepared for any surprise or danger."

Then he spoke to Flor de Ángel: "Especially you, because you're a very pretty young girl. Be very careful, because the smugglers could rape you along the way. If you had gone with me, you would have been well protected. But you've decided to change your plans, and you're risking your own lives to help this girl and her daughter. May God bless you."

The man was honest and, so that we could pay another guide, returned the part of our payment that was for the border crossing and transportation to our final destination in the United States.

The group left, leaving us completely alone. Suddenly I realized the seriousness of the guide's words. I decided to proceed with great caution from then on, but I tried not to let Flor de Ángel see my concern, as I didn't want to worry her.

A short time later I went to the hotel office and called the number on the piece of paper. A man answered, and I explained our situation. He said he would come to the hotel in an hour, which he did, and he met with us in our room.

The smuggler looked like a hoodlum. He acted suspicious and did not inspire the least bit of confidence, but he was our only hope if we wanted to help Jimena cross the border with her daughter.

The man didn't beat around the bush, "I don't take people across by Tijuana," he said. "Only through Arizona, because there's less border patrol. But first we have to take care of the matter of money."

I gave him what I had gotten back from Moisés's friend, to cover the trip for Flor de Ángel and me.

The man took the wad of bills and counted them. He smiled strangely and asked Jimena, "Who's paying for you and the baby?"

"My husband."

"Where is he?"

"In Oregon."

"I need his name and phone number. If he pays my contacts in the United States today, we'll leave tomorrow. So be ready."

Jimena gave the man the information. Without any further explanation, he left the room. Jimena was happy. She picked up Amanda and said, "We'll be with your daddy soon."

Amanda smiled.

# 37

Early the next morning, the smuggler knocked on the door of our room and said, "It's all set. Have breakfast and get ready to leave. I'll meet you at the door in an hour."

An hour later, we joined a group of nine other travelers and got on a minibus, which immediately pulled away from the hotel and sped through the deserted streets on the outskirts of Tijuana.

The smuggler told us, "We're heading for Caborca, Sonora. From there we'll take another bus straight to the Arizona border."

In Caborca, we bought food and water. Then we traveled the second leg of the journey. The Arizona border was desolate and extremely hot. The radio on the bus announced that the temperature would reach 110 degrees that day, expected to be one of the hottest days on record for the month of May. In Caborca, we had been told to buy cotton caps to protect ourselves from the sun, and enough water.

"In case you didn't know," the smuggler said, "we'll be crossing the border through the desert. So get ready for a little bit of sun."

The vehicle stopped and we got out. The sun was beating down, and the heat was so intense that it felt like we were entering an oven.

"We're going to roast," said Flor de Ángel.

Jimena was worried about Amanda and covered her little head with a cap. The baby began to cry, but Jimena soothed her by giving her some water to drink.

The smuggler gathered the group and said, "This is the border. That's Arizona. We'll walk straight from here toward a town called Sells. There, we'll be picked up by a bus that will take us to Tucson. Follow me and remember: don't stray off the path. And don't fall behind or you'll get lost."

The guide set off across the desert and we followed him. The heat was so intense that even after walking a mile, my body had not adjusted to the temperature. To conserve water, we drank only small sips, just enough to avoid extreme thirst. But little Amanda could not stand the heat, and she cried as Jimena and Flor de Ángel comforted her as best they could.

After walking several miles, we stopped under the shade of a small tree, that was really just a bush. We had lost sight of the guide and the rest of the group, and we believed they were ahead of us.

"Let's hurry," said Flor de Ángel. "Otherwise, they'll leave us behind and we'll get lost."

"I don't feel well," Jimena moaned. "Everything looks blurry and I feel sick to my stomach."

I took Amanda in my arms, and Flor de Ángel helped Jimena, who began to vomit.

"Let's go on," I insisted, trying to spot the others in the distance. But all I could see was sky and desert, bright and blinding under the sun's rays, which by now were burning our skin like flames.

I had the horrible feeling that we had been left behind. But I thought that if we kept going straight, we would reach the town where they would be waiting for us.

Jimena was moaning and walking very slowly, helped by Flor de Ángel, who despite the heat, thirst and fatigue had not lost heart. Amanda was sleeping in my arms.

I figured we must have walked between ten and fifteen miles. By this time, Jimena's condition had worsened, and she was refusing to go on. We had consumed nearly all the water. All that was left was a third of Amanda's bottle, and Amanda was not waking up. I assumed she had fallen into a deep sleep.

As we pressed on, we came upon a member of our group lying dead in a pool of dirty water. In his desperation, he had taken off all his clothes. I remembered that the guide had told us not to drink out of any pools, because the water was contaminated from poisonous reptiles. People would come to the pools, drink a great deal because of their immense thirst, and drown right there.

We found a little bush on the path and leaned against it to rest in its shade. I sat down, still holding little Amanda. Jimena, resting next to Flor de Ángel, was exhausted and said only "Water . . . water." She appeared to be near death.

When she regained consciousness for a moment, she said in a failing voice, "Promise me you'll take care . . . of my daughter. . . . For God's sake, promise me."

Flor de Ángel murmured, "I promise."

"You too . . . sir," Jimena said to me.

"Yes, I promise."

"Now I can die . . . in peace," she said.

The sun was burning my skin, and the thirst was unbearable. I felt like I was being consumed by an intense fire. Flor de Ángel put out her hand, and I took it in mine. With my other arm I held little Amanda. Suddenly I felt as though my brain was disconnecting from the rest of my body and everything was dark, peaceful and silent. . . .

In the distance I saw a white figure approaching. It was Grandfather, bringing water, lots of water. He cooled our faces with it and gave us little sips to drink. He took little Amanda in his arms and kissed her forehead. The shade his figure provided protected us from the burning sun . . .

# 38

When I woke up, I was lying in a bed. I felt very weak and had a terrible headache and was very thirsty. One of my arms was full of wires that were connected to a machine and a bottle of clear liquid. To my right was Flor de Ángel in the same situation, still asleep. To my left, in a crib, was little Amanda.

A nurse came over to me and said, "You finally woke up."

"Where am I?" I asked.

"In a hospital, in Arizona. In the United States. You're the second one to regain consciousness. The first one was the baby."

"Flor de Ángel opened her eyes and moaned. Then she cried out, "Sergio! Sergio!"

"I'm here," I said.

She turned and looked at me as if to speak, but the nurse stopped her. "Rest. You need to regain your strength. You got here twelve hours ago, unconscious and dehydrated."

Flor de Ángel asked, "And the baby? Where's the baby?"

The nurse lifted Amanda from the crib.

"She's just fine. Very hungry, that's all."

"And Jimena?" I asked.

"The others are in the next room."

"How did we get here?" Flor de Ángel wanted to know.

"It's nothing short of a miracle that you were found in the desert," the nurse explained. "The Border Patrol report says that you were found lying under a bush and brought here immediately by helicopter. They found twelve adults and the one little girl. Two men and one woman had already died."

An officer came into the room and, after looking around, spoke to the nurse in English. "Tell them they'll stay here a few days until they feel better and that then they'll be turned over to Immigration."

I told the officer that I spoke English and that I was very grateful that they had saved our lives.

"How is it that you speak English so well?" the nurse asked me.

"I came to the United States when I was six."

"How old are you now?" asked the officer.

"Sixteen."

"And your parents, where are they?" he asked.

"In Los Angeles."

"Are you undocumented?"

"No, I'm a resident. My parents are U.S. citizens."

"And what the hell were you doing risking your life in the desert?" he asked angrily.

"It's a long story," I replied.

"Okay," said the officer. "When the doctor releases you, we'll see what Immigration has to say."

The officer and the nurse left the room. I explained everything to Flor de Ángel.

"Are they going to deport me?" she asked.

"I don't know. I hope not!"

"And what's going to happen to Jimena and Amanda?"

"I don't know that either. The important thing is that we're alive."

Flor de Ángel closed her eyes and fell asleep. Little Amanda was playing in her crib. Another miracle had occurred in my life and had saved me from dying in the desert. Then I remembered the dream in which Grandfather was rescuing us. I thought that maybe it was real.

"Thank you, Grandfather, for protecting your grandson, and for giving him so much love," I whispered.

# 39

As soon as I felt better, I contacted my parents and my school counselor at Belmont High. As was to be expected, my father was furious and very upset at all the problems I had gotten myself into. My mother was just happy that I had survived that very dangerous trip. Mrs. Berenson couldn't believe everything that had happened to me, and as usual was willing to help me in any way she could.

An immigration agent came to the hospital to explain the situation to us. The most complicated situation was little Amanda's. Jimena, her mother, had died in the desert, and there was no one to take care of her. Then I remembered that Jimena had given us the name and phone number of her husband in Oregon. I called him and told him the sad news. He cried bitterly and said that he would travel to Arizona immediately to pick up his daughter.

Two days later, Amanda's father arrived at the hospital. He identified his wife's body and provided all the information that Immigration required. The man was disconsolate and felt defeated. His dream had been to start a new life with his wife and daughter in the United States, but now one of them had been taken from him. But little Amanda was so full of life and smiled so much that she inspired her father to continue his struggle. He decided to bury Jimena in their homeland and leave the little girl with her grandparents. He would return to Oregon to work hard in order to give his daughter a better life, in memory of Jimena.

Flor de Ángel's case was not too complicated. With the help of a community organization in Arizona, her deportation was avoided and she was set free for six months with a low bond. During that time, we would find a way for her to remain legally in the United States.

My case was the least complicated of all because I was already a legal, permanent resident of the United States. I received a serious reprimand from the Border Patrol and the Immigration judge for entering the country illegally. I promised never to do it again.

The rest of the survivors were deported to their home countries, except three of them who applied for political asylum with the assistance of the same organization that helped Flor de Ángel.

So finally, one morning Flor de Ángel and I left the hospital for the airport to catch the plane that would take us to Los Angeles, to my parents' home.

# 40

Flor de Ángel joined our family as an adopted daughter, and was able to win over my parents and my friends. What made my father very happy was that, with Flor de Ángel's help, we were able to clean a larger building for our night job, which allowed us to earn more money. Flor de Ángel adapted to life in this country and learned English quickly. She also attended Belmont High School, and both of us planned to go on to college after graduation.

Flor de Ángel and I conducted ourselves as great friends, but we had sworn to love each other forever. She was the most beautiful, intelligent, wonderful girl I had ever met. She did not allow herself to be dazzled by the material things in this country, like many young people I knew. As a song Grandfather liked says, "Money isn't life; it's just vanity." He said there were more important things, like peace, love, and friendship, and that money couldn't buy those things.

Someday, after Flor de Ángel and I graduate from college, we will get married and have our own family. That's our dream. I'm sure that Grandfather will help us make it come true. He always showered me with blessings, and I know he'll never let me down, because dead or alive, he is a wonderful grandfather.

# 41

Later on, when Flor de Ángel and I had completely recovered from the trip and our lives had returned to normal, Mrs. Berenson asked me to tell her all the details of the events of my adventure.

It amazed her so much that she said, "I think that somehow your story should be told to the students and teachers at Belmont High, and even to those at other schools. It would help them become more familiar with the conditions of poverty in which people live in other countries. They would understand that this forces them to leave their homelands and come to the United States. It is also important for them to know the great difficulties people go through to get here.

"I think your story would help the Latino community learn more about its own history, and would help the broader community understand more about the immigrant experience, especially the very difficult experience of young people, their efforts to adapt to this culture, their ideals of fulfilling their dreams of a better life. With your story, the positive features of the community and its contributions to this country would be better understood."

I commented to the counselor that sometimes at school there was tension between newly arrived students and those who had come to this country a long time ago or were born here to immigrant parents.

"I understand," she said. "And perhaps this story may also help create harmony among those young people who, sometimes because of the conflicts typical of their age, feel embarrassed because of their roots and their language, or because of their status as immigrants."

"Maybe so," I said.

The counselor added, "I even believe that this story could help young Latinos resolve their identity problems and improve their self-esteem. I also believe that it would spark young people's interest in reading, something they don't do enough of because there are not many books of interest to them that reflect their own reality, with characters with whom they can identify."

❧    ❧    ❧

So it was that, with the help and enthusiasm of Mrs. Berenson and several teachers and students at Belmont High, we managed to compile this story that we decided to call *A Promise to Keep,* which you, dear reader, have just read. I hope that you have enjoyed it. Thank you very much.

—Sergio

# About the Author

**M**ario Bencastro was born in Ahuachapán, El Sal-vador, in 1949. His first novel, *Disparo en la cate-dral*, was chosen from among 204 works as a finalist in the Novedades-Diana International Literary Prize 1989 in Mexico, and was published by Editorial Diana in 1990.

In 1993 his short story collection *Árbol de la vida: Historias de la guerra civil (The Tree of Life: Stories of Civil War)* was published in El Salvador by Editorial Clásicos Roxsil. The collection was written between 1979 and 1990, and several of its stories have been chosen for inclusion in international anthologies.

"Photographer of Death" and "Clown's Story" have been adapted for the stage. The latter was translated into English for the anthologies *Where Angels Glide at Dawn: New Stories from Latin America* (HarperCollins 1990) and *Turning Points* (Nelson Canada 1993). "Photograph of Death" is included in *Texto y vida: Introducción a la lite-ratura hispanoamericana* (Harcourt Brace Jovanovich 1992) and in *Vistas: Voces del mundo hispánico* (Prentice Hall 1994). "The River Goddess" is part of *Antología 3 X 5 mundos: Cuentos salvadoreños 1962–1992* (UCA Edi-tores, San Salvador 1994). "The Garden of Gucumatz" first appeared in *Hispanic Cultural Review* (George Mason University 1994).

Arte Público Press published English and Spanish editions of *A Shot in the Cathedral (Disparo en la catedral)*, *The Tree of Life: Stories of Civil War (Árbol de la vida: Historias de la guerra civil)*, *Odyssey to the North (Odisea del norte)*, and now *A Promise to Keep (Viaje a la tierra del abuelo)*.

*Odyssey to the North* was also published in 1999 by Editorial Sanbun of New Delhi, India.

# Additional Young Adult Titles

*A School Named For Someone Like Me*
Diana Dávila Martínez
2004, Trade Paperback
ISBN 1-55885-334-0,$9.95

*Across the Great River*
Irene Beltrán Hernández
1989, Trade Paperback
ISBN 0-934770-96-4, $9.95

*Alicia's Treasure*
Diane Gonzales Bertrand
1996, Trade Paperback
ISBN 1-55885-086-4, $7.95

*Ankiza*
Gloria Velásquez
2000, Clothbound
ISBN 1-55885-308-1, $16.95
Trade Paperback
ISBN 1-55885-309-X, $9.95

*¡Aplauso! Hispanic Children's Theater*
Edited by Joe Rosenberg
1995, Trade Paperback
ISBN 1-55885-127-5, $12.95

*Bailando en silencio: Escenas de una niñez puertorriqueña*
Judith Ortiz Cofer, Trans.
Elena Olazagasti-Segovia
1997 Trade Paperback
ISBN 1-55885-205-0, $12.95

*Border Crossing*
Maria Colleen Cruz
2003, Trade Paperback
ISBN 1-55885-405-3, $9.95

*Call Me Consuelo*
Ofelia Dumas Lachtman
1997, Trade Paperback
ISBN 1-55885-187-9, $9.95

*Close to the Heart*
Diane Gonzales Bertrand
2002, Trade Paperback
ISBN 1-55885-319-7, $9.95

*Creepy Creatures and Other Cucuys*
Xavier Garza
2004, Trade Paperback
ISBN 1-55885-410-X, $9.95

*Dionicio Morales: A Life in
    Two Cultures*
Dionicio Morales
1997, Trade Paperback
ISBN 1-55885-219-0,$9.95

*Don't Spit On My Corner*
Mike Durán
1992, Trade Paperback
ISBN 1-55885-042-2, $9.50

*El dilema de Trino*
Diane Gonzales Bertrand,
Trans. Julia Mercedes Castilla
2006, Trade Paperback
ISBN 1-55885-458-4, $9.95

*Emilio*
Julia Mercedes Castilla
1999, Trade Paperback
ISBN 1-55885-271-9, $9.95

*Estrellas peregrinas: Cuentos
    de magia y poder*
Victor Villaseñor, Trans.
Alfonso González
2006, Trade Paperback
ISBN 1-55885-462-2, $9.95

*Firefly Summer*
Pura Belpré
1997, Trade Paperback
ISBN 1-55885-180-1, $9.95

*Fitting In*
Amlú Bernardo
1996, Trade Paperback
ISBN 1-55885-173-9, $9.95

*From Amigos to Friends*
Pelayo "Pete" Garcia
1997, Trade Paperback
ISBN 1-55885-207-7, $7.95

*The Ghostly Rider and Other
    Chilling Stories*
Hernán Moreno-Hinojosa
2003, Trade Paperback
ISBN 1-55885-400-2, $9.95

*A Good Place for Maggie*
Ofelia Dumas Lachtman
2002, Trade Paperback
ISBN 1-55885-372-3, $9.95

*The Girl from Playa Blanca*
Ofelia Dumas Lachtman
1995, Trade Paperback
ISBN 1-55885-149-6, $9.95

*Heartbeat Drumbeat*
Irene Beltrán Hernández
1992, Trade Paperback,
ISBN 1-55885-052-X, $9.50

*Hispanic, Female and Young:
    An Anthology*
Edited by Phyllis Tashlik
1994, Trade Paperback
ISBN 1-55885-080-5, $14.95

*The Ice Dove and Other Stories*
Diane de Anda
1997, Trade Paperback
ISBN 1-55885-189-5,$7.95

*The Immortal Rooster and*
*Other Stories*
Diane de Anda
1999, Trade Paperback
ISBN 1-55885-278-6, $9.95

*In Nueva York*
Nicholasa Mohr
1993, Trade Paperback
ISBN 0-934770-78-6, $10.95

*Juanita Fights the School Board*
Gloria Velásquez
1994, Trade Paperback
ISBN 1-55885-115-1, $9.95

*Julian Nava: My Mexican-*
*American Journey*
Julian Nava
2002, Clothbound
ISBN 1-55885-364-2, $16.95

*Jumping Off to Freedom*
Anilú Bernardo
1996, Trade Paperback
ISBN 1-55885-088-0,$9.95

*Lessons of the Game*
Diane Gonzales Bertrand
1998, Trade Paperback
ISBN 1-55885-245-X, $9.95

*Leticia's Secret*
Ofelia Dumas Lachtman
1997, Trade Paperback
ISBN 1-55885-209-3, $7.95
Clothbound, ISBN 1-55885-
208-5, $14.95

*Looking for La Única*
Ofelia Dumas Lachtman
2004, Trade Paperback
ISBN 1-55885-412-6, $9.95

*Lorenzo's Revolutionary Quest*
Rick and Lila Guzmán
2003, Trade Paperback
ISBN 1-55885-392-8, $9.95

*Lorenzo's Secret Mission*
Rick and Lila Guzmán
2001, Trade Paperback
ISBN 1-55885-341-3, $9.95

*Loves Me, Loves Me Not*
Anilú Bernardo
1998, Trade Paperback
ISBN 1-55885-259-X, $9.95

*The Making of a Civil Rights*
*Leader: José Angel Gutiérrez*
José Angel Gutiérrez
2005, Trade Paperback
ISBN 1-55885-451-7, $9.95

*Maya's Divided World*
Gloria Velásquez
1995, Trade Paperback
ISBN 1-55885-131-3, $9.95

*Mexican Ghost Tales*
Alfred Avila
Edited by Kat Avila
1994, Trade Paperback
ISBN 1-55885-107-0, $9.95

*My Own True Name*
*New and Selected Poems for*
*Young Adults, 1984-1999*
Pat Mora, Drawings by Anthony
Accardo
2000, Trade Paperback
ISBN 1-55885-292-1, $11.95

*Nilda*
Nicholasa Mohr
1986, Trade Paperback
ISBN 0-934770-61-1, $11.95

*Orange Candy Slices and*
*Other Secret Tales*
Viola Canales
2001, Trade Paperback
ISBN 1-55885-332-4, $9.95

*The Orlando Cepeda Story*
Bruce Markusen
2001, Clothbound
ISBN 1-55885-333-2, $16.95

*Pillars of Gold and Silver*
Beatriz de la Garza
1997, Trade Paperback
ISBN 1-55885-206-9,$9.95

*Riding Low on the Streets of*
*Gold: Latino Literature for*
*Young Adults*
Ed. Judith Ortiz Cofer
2003, Trade Paperback
ISBN 1-55885-380-4, $14.95

*Rina's Family Secret*
Gloria Velásquez
1998, Trade Paperback
ISBN 1-55885-233-6,$9.95

*Roll Over, Big Toben*
Victor Sandoval
2003, Trade Paperback
ISBN 1-55885-401-0, $9.95

*The Secret of Two Brothers*
Irene Beltrán Hernández
1995, Trade Paperback
ISBN 1-55885-142-9, $9.95

*Silent Dancing: A Partial*
*Remembrance of a Puerto*
*Rican Childhood*
Judith Ortiz Cofer
1991, Trade Paperback
ISBN 1-55885-015-5, $9.95

*The Skyscraper that Flew and
    Other Stories*
Jesús Salvador Treviño
2006, Trade Paperback
ISBN 1-55885-444-4, $14.95

*Spirits of the High Mesa*
Floyd Martínez
1997, Trade Paperback
ISBN 1-55885-198-4, $9.95

*The Summer of El Pintor*
Ofelia Dumas Lachtman
2001, Trade Paperback
ISBN 1-55885-327-8, $9.95

*Sweet Fifteen*
Diane Gonzales Bertrand
1995, Trade Paperback
ISBN 1-55885-133-X, $9.95

*The Tall Mexican:
    The Life of Hank Aguirre,
    All-Star Pitcher, Businessman,
    Humanitarian*
Bob Copley
1998, Trade Paperback
ISBN 1-55885-294-8,$9.95

*Teen Angel*
Gloria Velásquez
2003, Trade Paperback
ISBN 1-55885-391-X, $9.95

*Tommy Stands Alone*
Gloria Velásquez
1995, Clothbound
ISBN 1-55885-146-1, $14.95
Trade Paperback
ISBN 1-55885-147-X, $9.95

*Trino's Choice*
Diane Gonzales Bertrand
1999, Trade Paperback
ISBN 1-55885-268-9, $9.95

*Trino's Time*
Diane Gonzales Bertrand
2001, Clothbound
ISBN 1-55885-316-2, $14.95
Trade Paperback
ISBN 1-55885-317-0, $9.95

*The Trouble with Tessa*
Ofelia Dumas Lachtman
2005, Trade Paperback
ISBN 1-55885-448-7, $9.95

*Upside Down and Backwards*
Diane Gonzales Bertrand
2004, Tradeback
ISBN 1-55885-408-8, $9.95

*Versos sencillos / Simple Verses*
José Martí, Trans. Manuel A.
Tellechea
1997, Trade Paperback
ISBN 1-55885-204-2, $12.95

*Viaje a la tierra del abuelo*
Mario Bencastro
2004, Trade Paperback
ISBN 1-55885-404-5, $9.95

*Walking Stars*
Victor Villaseñor
2003, Trade Paperback
ISBN 1-55885-394-4, $10.95

*White Bread Competition*
Jo Ann Yolanda Hernandez
1997, Trade Paperback
ISBN 1-55885-210-7, $9.95

*The Year of Our Revolution*
Judith Ortiz Cofer
1998, Trade Paperback
ISBN 1-55885-224-7, $16.95

*...y no se lo tragó la tierra*
Tomás Rivera
1996, Trade Paperback
ISBN 1-55885-151-8, $7.95